I0682868

GOLD MAN REVIEW

Gold Man Review is published annually by Gold Man Publishing.

The editors invite submissions of previously unpublished works of fiction, nonfiction, and poetry. Manuscripts can be submitted at www.goldmanpublishing.com by following our submission guidelines.

Address all requests to:
Heather Cuthbertson
Editor-in-Chief
Heather.Cuthbertson@GoldManPublishing.com

Contents

Issue 10 Editor's Letter

Welcome to a very special issue of *Gold Man Review*. Despite all the craziness that this year has brought, we have cause to celebrate because it's Gold Man's 10th issue. This is a huge milestone for a little journal that sprung out of an educational requirement. I'm completely in awe at the fact that it has made it this far, especially when the odds have been against it. These last ten years have, no doubt, been some of the most tumultuous ones in my existence and yet, ever present in the background, has been this journal. It has seen me through graduate school, a divorce, a move to a new state, a new marriage and all the wedding planning that went into it, three difficult pregnancies, three births, three busy children, the death of both my parents, the near loss of my home in the Carr Fire, and then finally the Covid-19 pandemic.

Like everyone, I've grown and changed in the last decade and so has Gold Man. It has expanded from publishing writers from Salem and the Greater Salem, Oregon areas, to opening its pages for writers in all of Oregon, to hitting the entire West Coast in Issue 4 where it has remained and will continue to stay. The West Coast is our vibe, and this is what best represents us. Even so, I'm excited to find out what is in Gold Man's future. I do have my hopes.

While I have acted as its guardian in a way, Gold Man wouldn't be here if it wasn't for its volunteers. In its decade-long existence, it has had many talented and experienced writers serve as its editors and readers, for which I am incredibly grateful; and this wouldn't be a celebration if they didn't get to share their own experience being part of *Gold Man Review*:

Marilyn Ebbs
Gold Man Review Issue 1-8

Working with Gold Man taught me so much about good writing and great writers. Every editor I had the pleasure of working with brought something unique to the table and we all respected each other's strengths and appreciated different opinions. And when you think of Gold Man, of course you think of Heather. Gold Man was her baby, and she is the reason each of us gave our best. She expects greatness from the authors, from the editors, and from herself. Thanks Gold Man for ten wonderful years. You earned it.

Lois Rosen
Gold Man Review Issue 3-4

The gleaming pioneer statue on the top of the Oregon State Capitol Building, nicknamed the Gold Man by locals, carries an axe to begin building a home in beautiful Salem. The energetic, talented editors of first *Gold Man Review* through their determination, enthusiasm, and love created a stellar literary home for poets and prose writers in yearly hundred page-plus journals, beginning in 2010 and continuing to this day. I had the joy of joining them in reading submissions the first years. Bravo, Heather Cuthbertson, Nicklas Roetto, Richard Beckham, Marilyn Ebbs, Darren Howard, and volunteers for developing such a superb magazine.

Darren Howard
Gold Man Review Issue 1-9

I am so happy I had a chance to play a part in editing the first few years of *Gold Man Review*. Heather came to our writers' critique group one day with this crazy idea. She was going to start a literary journal. We were all excited to play a part in it, but it didn't seem real at first. It never would have been real, either, if Heather hadn't poured her heart and soul into making it happen. For the first couple of years we worked out of different coffee shops around Salem, reviewing manuscripts, investigating the publication options, working on the design, and proofreading. It was a lot of work and a lot of fun, and we made a great team. I'm so glad to know Gold Man is still going strong, and proud that I helped make it happen.

Geri Copitch
Gold Man Review Issue 9-10

I have had the pleasure of being a reader for *Gold Man Review* for the past two years. Each time I look forward to diving into the diverse stories and poems sent our way. Reading for Gold Man nudges me to read in genres I don't normally pick up. I'm often impressed with the imagery poets are able to convey using a brevity of words, and marvel at the life experiences our non-fiction contributors submit. And of course,

I enjoy a good piece of fiction! It is an honor to read these little pieces of fellow writers' souls.

Richard Beckham
Gold Man Review Issue 2

I joined the GMR team shortly after receiving my MFA (and a complimentary coffee mug) to proclaim a piece of land under the flag of my own art. My time with GMR let me see other artists who, like me, set out with ink and pen to draw their plots and raise their flags as high as they could. Seeing myself as one of countless many on this rugged, fertile landscape was a multi-dimensional survey of myself and my fellow writers. As managing editor for one issue, I helped decide whose hopes must stake their plots elsewhere and whose flag we would help raise a notch. It was difficult but eye-opening, like the reward any pioneer earns after entering uncharted territory and pressing on. And, like any pioneer who desires to raise the highest flag, it was an experience that made me wiser and thankful that I'm not alone out there, riding toward mountains and the coastal cliffs beyond.

Ashley Rich
Gold Man Review Issue 6-10

I've been reading and editing for Gold Man for several years, and have read so many great stories, and of course, some not so great. But, during my first year, one story stood out, and has stuck with me all these years later. It, unfortunately, wasn't accepted as it didn't quite fit the Gold Man tone. But here's the thing, I think about that story a lot. I don't remember the title, or the author, but I remember how it made me feel, and the genuine delight it ignited in me. And in the end, that is what makes a great story. To the author of the Food Poisoning Barnes and Noble Customer story, I still think about you. I said all that to say this, don't ever take a rejection personal. I'm sure somewhere out there, a journal editor is thinking about your story and what else you might have written that they are missing out on. Thank you to ALL our past and future contributors.

Nancy Dobson
Gold Man Review Issue 9-10

I've been submitting my work to publications since the 90's, so I'm familiar with the thrill of acceptance and the disappointment, or sometimes just resignation, of rejection. Having the opportunity to be on the other side, and read submissions, has given me a new perspective on writing. As a reader, I'm looking for writing that stands out, resonates, and makes me feel a connection to the world. I take the aesthetic and mission of *Gold Man Review* very seriously, so the work has to impress me. But it's also thrilling to read a piece that touches me personally, one I'm excited to champion. Our team works tirelessly to compile each edition. It truly is a labor of love! For me personally, this experience has made me feel more connected to the writing community. On both sides of Submittable, we are all here because we have stories to tell. It's a privilege to help other writers share theirs with the world.

Sandra McDow
Gold Man Review Issue 2-3

On a rainy evening in a Salem coffee shop, I sat with a handful of other local writers and listened to Heather's vision ... a journal that would afford local and regional writers the opportunity to showcase their work and encourage the art. That night, the seed was sown, and with collaboration, hard work, and perseverance it came to fruition.

The *Gold Man Review* ... what a trip.

Being an associate editor in Gold Man's early days was truly a gift. It broadened my knowledge of differing world views, belief systems, and human behavior, and of differing techniques that work, or don't work, within a narrative—all tools for my personal toolkit.

I'm a better writer today from the experience, so thank you, Gold Man, and happy birthday.

Nick Roetto
Gold Man Review Issue 1-10

Gold Man Review was a dichotomy. Pain and pleasure existing simultaneously, like contradicting opposites. Many times, it was a puzzle without all the pieces. Other times, all the pieces fit as if it were a puzzle of one. In the end, *Gold Man Review* has taught me that success is only obtainable with an amazing team. Without the great vision and unique perspectives of every individual involved, we wouldn't be thinking about Issue Eleven.

Rachel Lofton
Gold Man Review Issue 1-2

Being a part of Goldman Review helped enlighten me to the joys of editing. I am so thankful I was able to be a part of such a fun and hard-working group! It was a privilege to enjoy working alongside these incredibly talented people. Work seemed more like play, which means it was chock full of good memories.

Daniel Link
Gold Man Review Issue 7-10

Since I came aboard the Gold Man team in 2017, I've read thousands of short stories, essays, and poems. They come to us in all levels of proficiency, from authors ranging from 14 to 90. The one constant is the need to say something, the message inside the writer that's busting to get out. I've learned a lot from the stories that have crossed my desk, and although most never make it in the journal, many have stuck with me. It's not an easy thing, putting your work out there for an editor to consider, and I'm grateful for the chance to read those messages, and to be a part of so many writers' journeys.

***

Thank you again to all of Gold Man's editors and readers over the years and thank you to its contributors. I feel extremely lucky to have been able to provide a place for so many to share their work and I'm proud to add that Gold Man has had the privilege of publishing many first-time authors who have gone on to have successful publishing careers. Above all else, *Gold Man Review* wouldn't have had such an amazing decade if it wasn't for its contributors. Thank you so much for believing in us.

Here's to another 10 years!

Heather Cuthbertson
Editor-in-Chief
Gold Man Review

Gold Man Review Editors
Issue 10

Heather Cuthbertson
Editor-in-Chief

Nicklas Roetto
Project Editor

Daniel Link
Editor

Ashley Rich
Editor

Geri Copitch
Editor

2020 Gold Man Review Readers
Nancy Bennett
Alex Von Dachenhausen

Five Kinds of Quiet
halina duraj

You have been up all night preparing. When I arrive, you say you are not done; there is still a freezer in the living room, ladders in the dining room, and on the tour of your house I am not allowed in the garage.

You say you need new sheets, and a mattress pad, and a stand-up fan. It's only the second time I've been in your house in almost two decades, but together we go to Target. Like an old married couple, you say, smiling.

In the mattress pad aisle, everything is waterproof; you say we don't need that yet. We agree on sheets, patterned but no flowers, 400 thread count good enough. What would 700 be like, we wonder? Would we slide off them?

We choose the pricier stand up fan—because your son still has two years in high school and where you live is hot, unlike where I live. The fan offers "five kinds of quiet." We undress, then assemble the fan. It has a remote control and I sit on the edge of your bed, naked, cycling through Sleep, Calm, White Noise, Refresh, Power Cool.

In the morning I meet your son, who didn't exist when I was last in your house, and you sit in your dining room at your computer and fill out forms for your son's Robotics Club trip, and I sit at your dining room table where so many years ago you and your wife-at-the-time had a dinner party and I couldn't eat the quiche. I was too nervous; it was you across the table. You, whom I loved quietly, secretly. Not even you knew that I loved you.

That was before I disappeared and before your marriage faltered and before you found yourself alone and before you knew I loved you and before you started to love me back and before you found me again halfway around the world so that I could come back and find you and both of us could be happy.

What a story, we say again and again. Will anyone believe it? It doesn't matter.

Your house is different than I remember it. Also the same. The table is oriented differently. "You sat there," I say, thinking of the quiche. "I sat here." I touch the back of the chair.

I sit again at the same oval table, and I write this here as you sit there and write whatever you're writing, and your son lies on the couch ten feet away and plays a video game—samurais, knights, Vikings, all doing battle together, stratified by time, unified by weaponry. You ask him to turn it down a notch, a little quieter, so I can write, and he does.

You think I'm just being nice when I say the noise doesn't bother me, but you don't understand. How to tell you: those warriors grunting in battle, your son talking into his headset and the radio on low in the kitchen with the Christmas cactus I gave you twenty years ago that you have kept alive all this time—all of this makes the sixth kind of quiet, the best kind, in which I already thrive.

Drifting

claire scott

Can you feel it the slight drift
an almost lift of your feet
no longer as firm on the ground
hovering, not so certain of basics
like hospital corners on beds
or how to mulch the Tea roses
fewer phone calls, fewer texts
thinking of getting rid of your landline
and tossing your laptop filled with spam
a grandson no longer asks to play Scrabble
a frenzied daughter doesn't call asking
how to fix a too salty stew, or would an orange
sweater be OK for a first date
the neighbor nods and smiles, but doesn't ask
how to store bulbs over the winter
or would you take in her mail next week
when she goes to Nantucket
can you feel it
can you feel your boat wafting a bit
wavering in the water
can you feel the almost imperceptible
drift into irrelevance

nonfiction

Binary Language
emily townsend

My hearing aid shrieked when you brushed your hand behind my ear during your first attempt to kiss me. I didn't want to tell you I was prelingually deaf; I hadn't even told my roommate until a week after living together.

I blushed from both shame and surprise. "I wear hearing aids, by the way."

"I still like you," you said. Your lack of hesitation quelled my fears of meeting someone who wouldn't want to handle it.

For the rest of the night, you kept trying to kiss me and, out of my virgin innocence, I was disgusted when your lips finally found mine as we stood by my bed. People enjoy kissing? This wasn't like the movies. Where was that glittering madness of melting into you, where was that urge to push through an untouched heart? I should've known then that your lips would become the very thing I'd miss.

"All right, a quick story about my husband, and then I need to finish reading this packet," my poetry professor digressed. "When John and I first started living together, he would peel me an orange every night. At first, I was too independent. I didn't need anyone doing anything for me. But he kept doing it. I later found out that chimpanzees show affection by peeling oranges for their mates."

Up until I heard this story, I believed affection was false, a sparkling film strip that only played inside my head. All the projects I turned into workshop were about broken relationships. Just months before my freshman year of college, my father had divorced his second wife. My ten-year-old self could see how they loved each other; my nineteen-year-old self couldn't see how love existed at all.

Prelingual deafness typically occurs through maternal infections, such as cytomegalovirus, rubella, toxemia during pregnancy, and maternal diabetes. There was no one in the Townsend/Garcia bloodline that had a deaf ancestor. I was soothed through my mother's tears dropping on my head, not from being her first and only girl, but from knowing I was the odd one out. I was this bundle of silence, watching for movement to follow rather than sound. I created worlds inside my name being called.

When I was two, my parents took me to a speech therapist in Seattle, which did not fix my inability to push th through my lips or trap my tongue in the bite of my teeth for zzzz. I knew how they should've sounded by studying the therapist's lips. But on some tired, cranky days, word association became paired with facial expressions. She must be saying a bad thing if she looked mad, or a funny joke if she grinned with her teeth showing. Sometimes I was the understudy, mimicking the lead backstage, practicing half-determined to copy the real thing.

As we drove through the sepia lights illuminating grungy cement in the Mount Baker Ridge Tunnel, I couldn't remember the sounds I attempted to recall, but the concrete proof of the word through a moving mouth. The nineteen miles to home, my mother would speak to me, try to repeat the lesson. I tossed out my words into the tunnel, rolling lisped consonants into Lake Washington.

You laughed when we learned I couldn't pronounce zoo.

" *Thoo?* "

"The *zoo!* "

" *Nuu?* "

"Zoo. Like where exotic animals live."

You kissed me. We hadn't said Those Three Words yet, but I could read your eyes that you wanted to say it.

There were other words we pronounced my way—"thocks," "seeuhbatta," "korghee"—and words that had a heavier weight, words that never should have left my brain. You adapted my speech pattern and distinctive statements, which honestly frightened me at first. There was no hard-of-hearing role model for me growing up, and suddenly I had become one for a hearing person. My dialogue was skewed, aberrant. I didn't know how to formally integrate into the hearing world, so I acted my way in. It amused me that you picked up when I wasn't paying attention when I said a deflated "yeah" and you laughed when I kept mangling words and said it correctly for me. You were fascinated with my impairment and still wanted to study me when no one else would look.

It was my third year taking classes with my poetry professor, and she repeated her orange story at the beginning of the semester. I took her husband's fiction workshop as well. He gave a huge variety of reciprocated love stories, stories about their daughter. They never seemed tired of each other. I finally began to think love was a present history, seen beyond pages and movies. Humanized glamorization. It would be another two years before our films collided.

Still, I kept imagining some false version of you, a man who was not 6'5", a man who I could serendipitously meet on campus—the library, perhaps, where I spent most of my days—a man who didn't know how to handle the more difficult parts of me. In my scenarios, my issues were away from my hearing and more grounded on my loneliness. I needed you to hold me during existential crises at four in the morning. I needed someone to talk to and not feel like I was overwhelming them.

For a while, my writing kept me company. I wrote letters to the thought of you. Created playlists for our drives in the country. Imagined us cooking dinner and running out to get ice cream. I'd never gone as far as introducing you to my parents, or where we'd live once I graduated college, or thinking about our kids. I just wanted the instant relief that you were there, somewhere in the crevices of my films, playing your role. It was selfish of me to impose these standards once I actually met you, but you turned the tables and imposed all this on me.

The very first day we started talking, I mentioned how I wanted to be proposed to on a ferry in Seattle. "I'm moving there someday," I warned, giving you the out in case you didn't want to pursue a complicated, long-distance relationship, even though we hadn't yet met in person.

"It looks very pretty there," you said, after Googling Seattle ferries. "I could see myself there with you."

Of all the things I could see, I couldn't see you.

Ever since I was old enough to consciously remember bad feelings, classmate snubs, and humiliation from mishearing and misanswering, I kept trying to dissimilate my disability, thus blocking out potential friends and relationships. My grip on studying body cues faltered when I wanted to get out of the conversation. In one instance, at the pizza restaurant I worked at during high school, a customer was either joking being angry or angry while joking, and I misread his face and laughed. He never came back.

These badly executed conversations burned me at night, and it made me warier the next day. Eventually, I gave up on talking to people first, stuck to the foolproof script of general chats, and excused myself as early as I could. No one wanted to dismantle my planned dialogue long enough for me to improvise and see where I landed.

Later on, after I started to become comfortable with the same people who rotated through workshops, I spoke up more often. I wasn't that quiet girl in the corner whose notes were only written on the page. I was noticed, and I realized that my professor waited until I was done cleaning a hearing aid before class to begin the discussion. He didn't want me to miss anything, and the small gesture weighed the heaviest.

The 2017 solar eclipse happened five days before my brother's wedding, where my parents hugged for the first time in twenty years. It was ten seconds, a full breath, a history book opened then shut. It almost hurt to watch. Like the sun embracing the moon, all the light whooshed out from the adorned atmosphere into my parents, whose arms were only going to hold on for a brief moment.

"Congratulations on our first son getting married," my father said after stepping back. My mother smiled. They spent the rest of the night avoiding each other while I spent the rest of the night bouncing between them, drowning in wine to forget how alone I was. There was love everywhere in that room. I danced with my brother while his wife danced with her brother. You were still a faceless body every time I imagined dancing with you. I wondered if my parents would hug again at our wedding.

I knew I loved you when I watched a couple hug goodbye at the TSA line in the Colorado Springs Airport. I first thought I loved you when you reached over me for your phone and I said, "It's Eastern… Middle Time?" and you collapsed on me laughing. We were barely a month into dating and my speech patterns revealed themselves while lying in bed, during brief rides to dinner, wandering the aisles in the grocery store. One night we made a chocolate-rich dessert of Reese's and marshmallows and when we couldn't finish it, you said, "We'll have to make this for our kids someday." You were thinking about our future way before I did, but you were the first person who imagined me in their future. You wanted me, even with my silliness, with my genuine confusion on how to pronounce certain words, with my frustrations that I wasn't like everyone else, and my fears of passing along my disability. The world didn't find me cute and funny growing up with my speech impediment—they found me awkward and treated me as invisible. I couldn't have our kids going through the same thing. You didn't know about my many nights beating myself up for some conversation that went wrong during the day, or how embarrassed I felt when I answered someone's "Can you press three?" with "I'm good, how are you?" in an elevator since I'm accustomed to a predetermined set of greetings.

But you still wanted me, in spite of all that. You didn't get annoyed when I tossed in bed for the fourteenth time while trying to sleep. You were patient when I couldn't understand you after a shower and my hearing aids were out. You kissed my forehead when I revealed some sad memory from childhood. All this meant even more to me than your acceptance of my impairment. It didn't burden you, so I didn't feel like a burden. We were a love story. I could finally say out loud that I had found someone who took all of me willingly.

My parents never showed affection when they were married. But, of course, I could have forgotten about it. I was seven when the divorce finalized. When they remarried other people, it was rare to catch some sort of sentiment in the act. One household had bouts of anger and sharp breaths, the secondary more focused on the kids than each other. When my parents had to exchange us on house curbs or after soccer and softball games—"Have them back by six," they reminded. During pivotal teenage years, I often got caught in the middle with snarky comments and back-stabs. They weren't the sole reason I couldn't trust relationships and the concept of love, but they sustained the most weight. I vowed if I ever got married, I wouldn't hate my spouse if we ever decided to separate. How could you hate who you once loved the most?

Seeing my writing professors still so in love with each other over the five years I took their classes made me realize that it was possible to keep the same person around for the rest of your life. There were other examples to follow, examples that were not directly personal. The things I saw on a screen appeared in real life, at airport gates waiting for a flight, in lines funneling into a concert. There were casual flirts walking out after work and grazed hands in bars swapping pool sticks. There were stories of a proposal in a truck after a cat died and stories of peeling oranges before bedtime.

I had never gotten close to a boy before like how we've gotten close. When you were on top of me and cradled my head in your palm, some-times you shifted my hearing aid. You made love to me anyway, chuckling at the normal occurrence. It never bothered you, the squeal, the instant withdrawal to plug it back in, or even in the morning, when I didn't have them in at all, you guided me rather than give up.

I spent a weekend at your parents' house, a few weeks after their twen-ty-fourth anniversary. They held hands and walked on the same side as we do. Though they sat separately in the living room, they carried an easy conversation over the television. Your aunts came to town for someone's birthday, and they looked at each other like they were the first flower blooming in the spring. And in the corner of the house, tucked in the loveseat, we snuck kisses and talked about your family, how everyone got along. That night, I told you about mine, how no one got along. You said you would never leave me or do that to our kids. We sat outside with your aunts drinking strawberritas and listened to frogs croak and sipped on humid East Texas air. The stars pulsed in the sky as I looked up beyond you.

We visited your grandparents the next day, and as they were telling me about how they used to have pet ostriches, I caught your gaze while you mouthed "I love you." I forgot to breathe for a second. Your face was so soft, a cinematic moment that read This Is A Fucking Big Deal. It was not the first time we said I Love You to each other, but the first time we said it silently. You knew I could hear silence better than sound. You stepped into my quiet world and understood where you were.

In the backseat of your dad's truck on the way to town, you mouthed it to me. As your mom talked in the kitchen, you mouthed it to me while opening a soda behind her. We easily could've said it out loud, but it was more special inside our universe.

Even after I moved 1700 miles away from you, we still kept up our lip-speech phrase. At the Dallas-Fort Worth airport after four days in Texas, you waited for me to get through the TSA line, watching me the entire time. I couldn't stop my tears. We looked at each other and mouthed "I love you." The atmosphere seemed to curve us into a vignette at that exact moment, where the stench of uprooted shoes diminished, where the crowd of huffy passengers walked away, where the focus was tight and tilt-shifted and eclipsed.

The TSA lady who checked my ticket noticed my red eyes and said, "You must be leaving someone you don't want to leave."

It only made me cry harder. I loved you so much it hurt to leave, but I didn't love you enough to stay.

Medium Rare

laura picklesimer

Bert is a difficult man. Some might call him an asshole or at best, simply obtuse. He doesn't have many friends; in fact, he has none, just a coworker who occasionally joins him for lunch at an overpriced cafe with open-faced sandwiches, but only if Bert pays. Bert excels at the mathematical: differential equations, perfect numbers, balanced spreadsheets. When he is nervous, his right hand shakes.

Bert works at Elite Enterprises from 9 AM to 6 PM, Monday through Friday. He lives in a stained, stucco apartment complex forty miles from the office, since rent is so much higher in the city: 3.74 times as much; he has calculated it many times. He takes the commuter train to work, and when he returns home each night, Bert eats two heated Easy Gourmet meals. One is more than enough calorically, and his nightly overconsumption shows, particularly across his midsection and the soft undercarriage of his belly.

Bert recently purchased a MEbot, 9th edition. It is the same as the 8.5 model, but the color is a gunmetal gray rather than the alabaster sheen of the older version. Most people wouldn't notice, but Bert does.

He's a traditionalist when it comes to tech releases, so on the morning that the new model debuts, he stands outside the factory shipment line at 5 AM, alongside three hundred other customers who all ignore each another. These trips are draining for Bert. It's hard for him to alter his daily routine, but the excitement of showing off the latest MEbot at work offsets his nerves. For a moment, standing in that line, he feels complete, satisfied.

Bert had hoped his co-workers would comment on the fresh contours of his new MEbot. They don't. Bert never turns the MEmento setting off, so he records every activity of his day, even when he masturbates alone in his desk chair at the end of each night. His MEbot is always on, always in his hand or placed neatly in the clear receptacle that attaches to his chest over his clothes, so he can perform his daily tasks. Most people turn the device off in compromising or intimate moments like bathroom breaks and work meetings, in a united act of societal decency. There are workplace rules about it deep in the recesses of the 350-page contract Bert signed when starting with the corporation, but no one bothers him about it.

The day he picks up his new MEbot, Bert keeps his device set to ME-mento through the daily account reports, through his bathroom break at the urinal, and through his conversation about a new digital scanner with an uncomfortable young intern who smiles throughout his monologue but keeps tugging her hair back behind a heavily pierced ear.

It is the new device that notifies Bert of a message on his Hit It account, the very first message he has received on the platform besides the Welcome! email and weekly reminders to upgrade to Deluxe to check out young, willing babes within a fifty-mile radius. Bert is sitting down on his couch with a second plate of heated chicken carbonara when the buzz alerts him.

Bert ignores the content of the message and heads straight to the sender's profile picture. It is a photo of a sunset. His chest sinks. Bert clicks on her account, finds only a few scattered photographs, mostly selfies, angled from the chest up. Her username is FabRed. She enjoys sunsets, English bulldogs, and wine.

Bert is not attracted to FabRed; he prefers young, bird-like women. Instead FabRed is his age and appears to rival his portliness, and this saddens Bert, who feels for unknown reasons that he could do better. By all self-reported accounts, she is a perfectly average forty-year-old woman. Except she is apparently interested in Bert. This is a big difference, one that doesn't come along often, so he reluctantly replies.

Bert now has a date set for Saturday, his first in over a year.

Bert selects a restaurant close to his apartment, with free parking and the cheapest wine list he can find. He has a selection of dishes ready to suggest; they all reside on the upper portion of the menu, in the section titled "Firsts."

Bert replaces the sheets and makes his bed. He ME-plays a conversation from yesterday when he helped a female colleague work the copy machine.

"It's jammed here," Bert had said, taking out the offending slip of paper contorted between the ink jets. The hero. Then his right hand had started its shaking. Bert catches a smirk slip out of the coworker (something he hadn't noticed in real time), so he flips off the memory card. Bert must often edit around these embarrassments, composing his own, cleaner narrative of the past.

He fast forwards to lunch alone at his desk, a close up of salmon sashimi with delicate slivers of avocado and fish eggs, glistening green on pale pink. The colors calm him. He settles on a brief conversation with his cubicle mate after lunch, a joke about tuna, distinctly sexual, a moment Bert replays three times but still does not fully understand.

Bert often does not get the jokes, the little jabs and spars of his other male co-workers, the flirtatious remarks of women, none of which are directed at him. He replays these overheard side conversations, dissecting them for a punchline, a purpose, the comedy behind it all.

On the night of the date, seated at a tiny candlelit table, Beatrice (FabRed's real name) quickly sabotages Bert's careful preparations and orders an entire bottle of expensive Merlot. Bert sputters, trying to explain that he hardly drinks.

"It's better this way," she says, toasting midair and taking a sip before Bert has even poured himself a glass. Bert starts to suspect that he may hate her. He hides his hand, shaking already, under the table.

"You set your MEbot to MEmento," Beatrice says, motioning to the clear nylon wrapped around his neck. Bert perks up, gives the metal of the device a reassuring stroke. He hopes Beatrice will notice that it's a ninth edition.

"Get in the way, don't they?" she asks.

"Never," he says.

"I feel like they're going out of style, that it's more en vogue to just live in the moment."

"I am living. And when I'm done being in the moment, I'll have the proof right here, ready."

"To each their own."

Bert bites his lip, calculating how quickly Beatrice will polish off the bottle if she continues drinking at her current rate. Beatrice asks for an order of pommes frites even though the steak she has picked out (way down at the bottom of the menu under the "Mains") already comes with a side of them. Beatrice asks for her steak well done, and Bert quickly corrects her.

"You don't want that. Medium rare is how steak is supposed to be eaten. Anything else is a waste of a meal."

"I like it cooked all the way through."

"But steak isn't meant to be charred. It's a fact."

"Thanks, but I'll have it well done." Beatrice directs this statement to the server, and the matter is settled. She hands the menu over and smiles at Bert.

"I'm excited for dinner. It's been at least a year since I've had a good plate of fresh fries," she says. "I hope they serve them nice and thick." Her wink between sips is lost on Bert, who has begun moving his morning's MEmentos over to his data cloud.

Beatrice grabs her purse and pulls out an outdated MEbot, a clunky device that simply stores photos and manages social media, with only one hour of recording capacity. She's eager to share photos of her bulldogs with Bert. She moves on to photos of filled wine glasses, special tastings she claims to have attended. If he was more astute, Bert would notice that the photos were staged in her apartment, dog crate in the background, wine glasses smudged. Bert hates both dogs and wine, barely looks as Beatrice continues scrolling past photo after photo. He doesn't pick up on the sadness on her face, that Beatrice is ashamed of the photos, that the pictures are not boastings but rather her insecurities laid bare, that she's just as lonely as Bert.

The fries arrive. They're thin and long, stacked like oiled matchsticks. Beatrice asks for extra ketchup before she's even sampled one on the plate. She slides three out from the pile.

"Yum. It must have been at least a year since I've had fries."

"You said that already," Bert says.

"What?"

"You said that already, that you haven't had fries in a year."

"I don't think so," Beatrice says.

"You did. It was right after you ordered your steak the wrong way."

"Did I?" Beatrice shrugs her shoulders, moving on to another fry. "That's funny, I don't remember."

Bert cues the MEbot. This particular exchange takes only eight seconds to locate. When Bert finds it, he punches the volume up, zooms onto Beatrice's face, her thin lips, as she utters the words exactly as he had insisted.

"Well, there you have it," Beatrice says. She has stopped eating, a fry bitten in half lying on the plate.

"You also told me your dogs' names twice," Bert adds. "I can find that, too."

"That won't be necessary," Beatrice says. She dabs at her face with her napkin, almost delicately. She places it on the table next to her plate.

"Excuse me," she says. Beatrice leaves for the back of the restaurant, disappearing under the bright restroom sign.

Every server in the restaurant realizes that Beatrice is not returning before Bert does, even the busboy in the back corner who didn't cover his section. But Bert receives his meal of roasted chicken and eats his entire plate. He finishes, and Beatrice has still not returned. Her overdone steak and fries sit there. Bert tries to drink as much of the wine as he can, but he hates its acidic bite. When he finally realizes what has happened, he asks for a to-go box.

On the way home, Bert calculates that he could have bought himself 37 prepackaged Easy Gourmet meals with the money he spent on the date.

After he changes for bed later in the night, Bert uses the MEbot to zoom in on a close-up of Beatrice's backside as she left the table. He uses the image to masturbate to in his clean, empty bed. Bert feels sick after. Both his hands are shaking, and he knows he's close to vomiting.

He spends an hour crouched over the toilet; his forehead comforted by cool porcelain. He has removed the MEbot as a precaution, keeping it next to him on the bathroom counter. Its one green eye flashes, records, remembers.

Bert comes back to bed and notices the new stain in the center of his bed. He looks down at his MEbot, still watching him. Bert decides to stop recording, just to see what might happen, only for a second. He presses OFF and sees the tiny green light dim and disappear. A wash of silence, a rush of nothingness, floods him. A pressure lifts. Both his hands are now still, steady.

Bert stares at his dark reflection on the screen, tempted to reach out a hand and turn the MEbot back on. But he decides to keep the device off for the night, to stay alone with his thoughts, alone with this unfamiliar feeling of shame. He knows that as soon as he awakens the next day, he will need to click that tiny circular button, start all over again, but in the meantime, this is an unexpected release, a tiny comfort. Bert closes his eyes and sleeps.

To(o) Intimate

jessica mehta

To intimate is to suggest I shouldn't (perhaps)
tell you *Give me prayer hands*   (*higher*)
so the ropes don't lash your face. (Bottoms, you see,
don't want rope burns on *those* cheeks
unless they asked for it
in advance). It's too intimate, they said,
using measuring tape
instead of hemp hank. I suppose
it's fine when doctors family   loved
ones friends   that one
celebrity   the blogger on IG
tells you you're the wrong kind
of thicc but inch by inch in *real life*
is too triggering for some. I'd like
to intimate, yet again, that *this*
is not mature/adult/triple-x content,
          this
is the human body   canvas   form
un-sheathed and *Does this look*
sexual to you? Nudity is to intercourse
and averted eyes as books are to madness
and mutiny. It's too intimate to intimate
that we are beautiful stripped and hog-
tied in public. Let me paint my experiences
in cinema red across crowning iliac
crests and count the seconds dripping fast
before they shut us down in shameful protest.

From Smut Writer to Peter Meter Reader:
How Writing Erotica and Studying Sex Offenders Healed My Own Trauma

sherry shahan

My ex-husband left me his stack of sleazy men's magazines: *Adam, Cavalier, Nugget,* and others. I thumbed through them, remarking, "Any idiot could write better than this."

Thus began a career producing erotic fiction. My short stories were tongue-in-cheek tales, written in first person from a female's perspective. "Long Balls and Driving Shafts" starred a pro golfer (my ex) and a cocktail waitress at a Podunk country club (the reason he dumped me).

It was the mid-1980s. Luckily, I have one of those reset buttons that allows me to go back in time. I got to know a few of my editors and publishers. Men who took me to out-of-the-way restaurants where we dined at small tables in dark corners, drank copious amounts of wine, and traded anecdotes about the publishing biz. One gentleman liked to tease me about my spelling. "You always type *necessary* with two *C*s and one *S*." This, years before spellcheck.

I wiggled into a tight cocktail dress for a holiday party at a swanky hotel in downtown Los Angeles, the sort Richard Gere frequented in *Pretty Woman*. Midway into the evening, Larry Flynt appeared in his wheelchair flanked by bodyguards.

I recognized Flynt's round face and nutmeg-color hair partly because I'd begun submitting short stories to the infamous magazine. I wish I'd had the moxie to introduce myself as a potential contributor, but his admirers were many. I kept mailing manuscripts and adding rejection slips to the corkboard wall in my den.

After my failed marriage I went back to Cal Poly to finish my degree in Social Sciences. A professor in my department told me about an opening for a research assistant at Atascadero State Hospital (ASH), near my home on the Central Coast of California.

"Call Dr. Richard Laws," he said, chuckling. "He's the psychiatrist in charge of, um, an interesting project."

Why would I want to work at a maximum-security facility built to house Mentally Disordered Sex Offenders (MDSOs)? I needed extra cash.

Besides, the position sounded intriguing, maybe even worthy of a story.

The hospital was an imposing building with a labyrinth of four-person dorms and private rooms. The walls were cinder block or poured concrete. The beds, basically thin sleeping pads on ledges. It seemed odd that some doors could be locked from the inside.

On the day of my interview, a bank of woolly clouds floated above the complex. Razor wire rolled across the top of fences high enough to inflict a nosebleed. Men and women, presumably employees, rushed to and fro clutching clipboards or briefcases. They looked clenched, serious.

I'd made an extra effort in how I dressed—not wanting to attract the attention of any of the thousand-plus in the all-male institution. My friends called them scumbags and sick fucks. But the staff was adamant. "This is a hospital, not a prison. These are patients, not inmates." Words shaping impressions.

I wore loose slacks and a plain Jane blouse buttoned to the neck. Little makeup. No jewelry. Dr. Laws looked much as I'd expected, almost a cliché. Eager, yet composed, with gray flecked hair and a manicured goatee. Wire-rimmed glasses and a white lab coat.

"Tell me about your short stories," he asked, and grew still, listening.

The exchange lasted about 40 minutes.

Among other things, Dr. Laws' pioneer work looked at interventions for deviant and harmful sexual behavior. I was tasked with writing four, two-page scripts, each with a different scenario from the perspective of a woman being attacked. It was important that my stories sounded like true accounts and not merely something made-up. A long-term research assistant recorded my scripts.

Dr. Laws played the audiotapes in a private room for rapists who'd volunteered to be in his study. Here, "volunteer" seemed a loaded word. Many, no doubt, participated as a way to show their willingness to change. I tried to strip from the experience my personal judgment of their motivation.

The doctor monitored his clients' physical responses, though at the time I wasn't sure what that meant. But the findings supported my suspicion: These men were turned-on by the script of a woman begging for mercy. The scenario in which the victim fought back deflated their desire.

I'd hoped the findings would be made public, splashed across tabloids at supermarket checkout stands. I'd been in several sketchy situations myself. Once cornered in a bathroom by the shit-faced husband of a friend who pinned me on the cold tile floor. Instead of calling for help, I *talked* him down.

Another time, I found myself locked inside my VW bug with a guy I'd met while out of town. He pressed me against the steering wheel, clawing at my clothes. I wanted to tell him I was sick, about to throw up on him, but he was a deaf-mute.

I screamed so loud the car shook, actually vibrated. The creep must've realized others in the parking lot could hear me, because he took off running. There were other incidents. Were these men rapists, repulsive swine, or both? I never knew.

In a weird way, I wonder if that's why I took a job to help sex offenders restore normalcy to their lives? Is it possible the men who assaulted me could have been helped by Dr. Laws' program? No way to know, of course.

Dr. Laws explained why he had to safeguard the findings of his study. A select group of volunteers in a controlled situation was one thing. But once released, they would be dealing with endless stimuli and factors that couldn't be controlled. Trying these strategies in the real world could be risky.

I was issued an ASH ID card and a panic button. The gizmo was black, about the size of a pack of cigarettes, and hooked over my waistband. I'd been told to push the button if threatened or assaulted. "A security guard will be there in a flash."

I pictured a guard bounding down a long corridor beneath barred windows to rescue me. At 5'3" and 110 pounds I could be in serious trouble before his key slid into the lock. Between 1984 and 1988, 209 employees suffered 236 injuries from attacks by patients. The ward nursing staff suffered 185 of the injuries.

Colleagues tried to shock me with tales of the most mental patients, like the guy who killed a woman by hooking electrodes to her nipples. Afterward, he had sex with her. Necrophilia: *Sexual intercourse with or attraction toward corpses.*

Ray Norris, one of two convicted "Tool-box Killers," had been committed to ASH. Designated criminally insane as a teenager, he'd been locked up and then released. Later, he and a friend kidnapped, raped, tortured, and killed five teenage girls in Southern California. They used common household items, such as pliers and ice picks.

One day, I recognized a patient, a guy who looked to be in his early twenties. We'd studied in the same hall near the college library, bought potato chips from the same vending machine. I remember being attracted by his shaggy blond hair and intrigued by the sadness in his eyes. *Maybe I should strike up a conversation with him?*

He'd been busted for crawling into the bottom of an outhouse at Montano de Oro State Park to wait for someone to crap in his mouth. I wondered if any of his friends had inklings of his fantasies? If they were aware of anything odd about him?

Lesson learned: Spotting ritualistic perverts is harder than you think. They stroll among us at farmers' markets and bookstores. They're rarely the stereotypical wild-eyed guys in trench coats.

I pressed a buzzer by the thick smoky-glass door at the rear of the lobby. The door slid open automatically, and once inside the small, rectangular room, closed with a *whoosh* behind me.

A guard checked me out in that all-too-familiar way from behind thick, protective glass. Then he inspected my ID. The door leading into the main part of the hospital receded, so the pair of doors were never open at the same time. In theory, this kept patients from escaping through the lobby.

Being *inside* the hospital unnerved me. The men all wore the same khaki pants and shirts, laminated name badges, and smelled like bar soap. Some hummed popular tunes under their breath. All stared with an abstract look in their eyes, shuffling down long halls, arms dangling at their sides. It was like a highway system with traffic flowing in opposite directions.

I couldn't tell a child molester from a serial killer. Perhaps they resembled one another because they spent years hunched over the same dining tables, like old married couples.

No one wore belts. This, I learned was to keep them from hanging themselves, although over the years, too many had succeeded by tying a bed sheet to their locker. I heard one patient strangled another the same way. Now I understood why a patient might want to lock himself in for his own protection.

Dr. Laws' laboratory consisted of three interlocking rooms, the thermostats all set too low. Scores of men's magazines were scattered on a table in the cramped waiting room. I scanned the table of contents for my by-line. I'd done the same thing at magazine stands in liquor stores. Until working at ASH, I hadn't thought much about how men might be titillated by my stories.

A bookcase held porn movies and videos of young kids in ordinary scenarios, playing at school or riding a bike. The irony wasn't lost on me. Sexual material used to teach sex offenders how to control sexual arousal.

A one-way surveillance mirror provided a visual into the lab itself. The equipment was mammoth, intimidating. Knobs, gauges, dials, lights. The official name is penile plethysmography or phallometry, developed by Kurt Freund in the 1950s to assess sexual or erotic preference for children versus adults.

How did it work? A transducer or a rubber band-like tube filled with mercury fit over the base of a patient's penis. Connected to the machine, it measured blood flow, which in turn determined the amount of sexual arousal.

Dr. Laws' patients were called clients. They came in separately and sat in a chair that could've been in a dentist's office. I set up either a video or slide show with pictures of young kids and fired up the machine as I'd been taught.

Once I entered the observation room, adjacent to the lab, the client unzipped his pants and put on the transducer. The machine hummed while a needle recorded the amount of arousal or lack thereof on a single strip of moving paper. We privately called it the Peter Meter.

A client might have a strong sexual arousal when shown a photo of a 5-year-old boy because that boy had certain physical characteristics, perhaps a certain posture or manner of looking away from the camera. When he saw a boy like that, he fantasized about him in a certain way, and these fantasies could turn him on.

I worked alone with these guys behind locked doors several times a week. It was an odd sensation, passing through a porthole into another person's psyche. I tried to remain detached, not to think too much about their crimes.

There were no threats, catcalls, or whistles. Just the opposite, the guys spoke in hushed tones, their eyes averted. I sometimes joked, "The guys don't bother me because I'm too old for them." I was in my late twenties.

Using the Peter Meter, along with psychotherapy, helped certain clients understand the how, when, and why they were getting excited in the first place. As the maxim goes, "Where there's a *will* there's a *way*." For successful treatment, there needs to be both will (a sincere dedication to change) and a way (applying what's been learned).

I believed there was hope for pedophiles that *truly* wanted to change—who wanted to be better than they were. It seemed logical that they could redirect their thoughts or rewire their brain to control their behavior. If they were taught to realize they were getting excited *before* being fully aroused.

Dr. Laws and his colleagues believed it was a hope worth fighting for.

A lot has been written about tracking pedophiles after their release to ascertain their chances of reoffending. Multiple factors affect recidivism rates, such as how data is collected, the length of follow up, and risk levels of the group being tracked.

There's no doubt patients find themselves in situations that threaten abstinence. Most studies cite the importance of offenders learning self-empowering strategies *before* being released. Anger management, for instance, social skills training, 12-step programs, surveillance systems, such as family members monitoring a patient's behavior, and so on.

What I once thought a bizarre college job actually became part of my own therapy and recovery. Even though I wasn't aware of it at the time, it helped me move forward in my personal life, and pushed my writing to go beyond sassy sex stories, delving into deeper, richer personal essays.

I eventually began working on adventure novels for pre-teens. My characters survive lightning strikes, falling through black ice, rogue glaciers, and more—all of which are metaphors for overcoming struggles in day-to-day life.

fiction

Is That Sweet?
zoë ballering

Two weeks ago, on a ledge below my windowsill, a barn swallow laid four speckled eggs no bigger than the cotton balls I use to clean my face.

"Oh Mariel, how sweet," my mother cooed over videochat. "It's a quarantine miracle."

She treats the eggs like a special dispensation—like some loving god has seen fit to send me company. But I am not impressed, because some people have partners or children or dogs and every day, perhaps without even knowing it, they touch another living thing. Whereas I have a studio apartment without even a houseplant to my name. Now the eggs have hatched and the living things within my sphere of influence are six. There are four babies and two adults, and the adults fly away when I open the window and the babies barely seem awake. If I stretched out my hand, I could reach them, but my mother reminds me not to touch.

In between bouts of copywriting, I get up and look at the babies. They lie entwined and catatonic, cupped in an orgy of contact, until their mother perches on the nest. Then they spring up, desperate to differentiate themselves. Their eyes bulge and their open mouths eclipse their bodies; their heads are too big for their thin necks and so they wobble back and forth. In two quick movements the mother vomits into their mouths and then reaches down to swallow the soft white wad that emerges from their bare pink bottoms. Audubon Online informs me it's a fecal sac.

"Is that sweet?" I demand after detailing the process to my mother.

"Of course it is," she answers. "All care is tenderness and all tenderness is sweet." She has the camera on her laptop angled so that I can only see the bottom of her face—her yellow teeth, her jowly chin. Nothing punctures her optimism, not a plague nor the consumption of a fecal sac.

At first I thought the chicks barely had the strength to lift their heads, but the more I watch, the more I realize that they control the wobbling—that they bash their siblings out of the way to partake in that life-giving vomit. They are trying to survive. They are trying not to waste away into piles of pink jerky. In the morning, I spread peanut butter on my toast and ponder them. Each of their brains must be the size of a lentil. With a brain like that, I doubt there's any room for sweetness. Hunger must be all they can feel.

On the news they talk about a plague that's six times more virulent than measles and fifteen times more deadly than the flu. Only the Essentials go outside—those important enough or privileged enough to receive the antibody treatment that allows them to move freely through the world. One hundred and thirty-three days ago, when they first sent me home from the radio station, I thought my livelihood might die. Everything was dying then—the restaurants, nail salons, and sporting events; the movie theaters, flash mobs, and fashion shows; the parks, the swimming pools, and all the people. There were so many people who died.

Instead I started writing more than ever. Now I get ten requests a day—shill this, shill that. Coax forth a pleasing nugget of capitalism in a sixty second ad. Make the message tighter in a thirty. Buy it online. Have it delivered. Whatever it is—it's something you need. "Gruff country voice," I write in the production notes, or "bubbly, feminine delivery."

When I am writing I cease to be Mariel and I switch back and forth between Mary and Ariel. Mary implies that an air purifier can protect your family from the plague. She insists that you need a push up bra to feel good about yourself when you've been home alone for several months; she claims that shipping your valuables to an online pawn shop is the smartest way to make your rent. Then Ariel comes in. She couldn't write a good ad to save her life, but she can render a sensational ad less loathsome. Mary the creator. Ariel the Backspace Queen.

I buy everything that Mary and Ariel sell. Why run the risk of missing out when there's nothing else to do? I sit in my office which is really just a corner of my studio and while I am writing I ready myself for the sharp beep of a package being scanned. Then I don my mask and rush to the door, but I can never catch the courier. Only the box remains. For a few days I delight in the novelty: a monogrammed eye pillow, gummies that Mary promised would make me thin, an immersion blender, a Hitachi Magic Wand, earrings made from the blue iridescent wing of a Filipino butterfly, fitness leggings, a Cajun spice set, and a blanket designed to look like a tortilla so that I can roll myself up and post a killer selfie using #quarantineburrito.

When I tire of these objects, I throw them in the garbage and then I knot the bag and leave it outside of my apartment. I sit in my office until Robbie, the maintenance man, comes tromping down the hall. Then I don my mask and rush to the door, but I can never catch him before he removes my fecal sac. I suppose that I could wait by the door and thereby guarantee our interaction, but in the end, I always chicken out. In the early days of the plague there was no discernible difference between having a body and being a vector of disease. Now they assure us that Essentials aren't infectious, but my own body hasn't quite adapted. I hyperventilate when I think of Robbie—half from excitement, half from the fear.

Robbie is the designated Essential for the whole apartment block. Sometimes I hear him using the industrial vacuum or coordinating with the couriers who bring us food and medicine and other vital purchases. Other than that, I don't know how he spends his time. The rest of the building has a better view. West faces the entrance, North faces the thoroughfare, and East faces the dumpsters. I imagine the residents like iron filings dragged to their windows by the overwhelming magnet of his body. Watch him open the door, walk down the sidewalk, deposit the bag. Whereas I, on the south face, overlook a barren parking lot where nothing stirs except the birds outside my window.

The living things within my sphere of influence are five. I call my mother weeping.

"Is that sweet?" I demand after I detail how the baby ceased to lift its head. For a while the other babies stepped on it and trod it down into the bottom of the nest, but then the mother or the father came, plucked up the body, and tossed it away. "A decomposing nestling might attract a predator," Audubon Online explains to me.

"Oh Mariel," she says. "They're just trying to protect their other babies."

My mother has angled her camera correctly, and I can see her whole head, including her comically uneven bangs. That was our ritual when I was growing up: every month, flush with confidence, she'd wind up butchering my bangs. After the final, fatal snip, when she stepped back to survey her handiwork, she'd always launch into the same soliloquy. "Oh world!" she'd cry. "Why am I me? Why can't I ever find my keys? Why can't I cut my daughter's bangs?"

I am talking to my mom while wrapped in the tortilla blanket—one of the novelties I kept, because I knew that it would make her laugh. I can see myself on camera in a little box at the bottom of the screen. The lower half of my face is covered in tears and snot. I gleam like the glossy finish on a table.

"Oh, shhhhh," my mother says. "It's okay to cry. You're not just crying for a baby bird, you're crying for everyone. You're crying for the world."

But I think I actually am just crying for a baby bird, or for some other equally dumb reason. I never want my mom to cut my bangs again, and yet I'm crying because she can't, or because there's too much Mary in me, or because the Filipino butterfly earrings are made from Filipino butterflies. I can't stop crying because I can't start crying for the right things, and that makes me cry even harder. I sop at my face with the edge of the tortilla.

Out the window, I see the three remaining babies. It is their sixth day of living. When the mother finishes her feeding and flies away, the babies lose their energy. They've each been straining upright, trying to be taller than their siblings, and now their heads sink slowly down as if they're already asleep. They collapse into a pile, each neck draped across another. They form an interlocking circle, like some kind of talismanic ordering that is meant to keep them safe.

I watch the mother groom the babies in the nest, parsing their pink flesh and snapping up the white mites that course across their bodies. She vomits up a spider and the tallest, plumpest baby eagerly receives the prize. It swallows the spider, but the long black legs poke out from its mouth like an accidental horror movie—the alien arachnid emerging from the tender body of the baby bird. It gulps and shakes its head to coax the spider down its gullet, but then gives up and collapses back to sleep. It has no sense of menace or impending doom—there's only space for hunger or exhaustion.

When the mother returns, the baby springs awake with the legs still sticking from its mouth. The mother swallow is not gentle—she uses her beak to jam the spider down the baby's throat. I sense a certain level of exasperation. It makes me gag a little just to watch it, though I'm sure my mother would defend the sweetness of the act.

I recall a rumor from my adolescence—how the high school boys, swollen with hormones, their knobbly Adam's apples nearly popping from their necks, devoted themselves to a bizarre masturbatory practice called the Stranger Technique. They would deaden one of their hands by jamming it between their mattress and boxspring, or they'd cover it with a couch cushion and have a buddy sit on that, or fall asleep with their hand beneath their head and wake eight hours later with the throb of morning wood. Then, when they masturbated, their numb hand would feel like it belonged to someone else.

In truth, I am not so interested in using the Stranger Technique for masturbation. I still have my Hitachi Magic Wand, which does a better job than any hand I've ever met—my own or someone else's. But there are other things I want. I practice speaking ads into dictation software while sitting on one of my hands. After an hour, when my hand is suitably numb, it presses my bangs flat like my mother used to do, or pulls down my earlobe and stabs an earring through the hole. The stranger pinches me on the shoulder to make sure that I'm paying attention, then traces the sweaty band of flesh beneath my breasts. Once I had a lover who used to touch all my moles in a specific order, as if my body were a bank vault and only he possessed the secret code. Now the stranger inputs sequences that open me. Another man I used to know would rest his hand on the back of my neck when we walked side-by-side—an act that irritated me because I read it as a signal of possession. Now all I want is for the stranger to steer from the node on the back of my neck, though I have nowhere to be and nothing to do except write these endless ads.

"At Heritage National Bank, we're here for you," dictates Mary. "That's why we're making *free* self-care webinars available through our online banking portal."

"Here at Heritage, our team of banking professionals briefly considered suspending maintenance fees on accounts that didn't meet the minimum balance," adds Ariel. "But when we say that we're here for you, we don't mean *here for you* here for you. We mean here for you like that scuzzy ex-boyfriend who texts to ask if you're doing okay and then never responds to your answer."

I watch Ariel's bitterness attach itself to Mary's glowing copy.

"Stop dictation," Mary shouts. "Delete word delete word delete word—"

"That's fine," says Ariel. "But can we stop pretending that webinars are the pinnacle of altruism?"

"*Free* webinars," says Mary.

They bicker over what constitutes generosity while numbness builds the stranger up inside of me. Only at the first touch do they quiet themselves—Mary abandoning all her gilded claims, Ariel all her futile protestations. Pinching, caressing, pressing, twisting, slapping, stroking, scratching—I do all of these things. I allow the stranger to reach down my throat with the brusqueness of the mother bird. At other times, when I am sick of being me, I sit on both of my hands. Then, when my numb right hand clasps my numb left hand, I find myself completely nullified. I stare at the words on my screen as the strangers take solace in each other.

When the babies were born, they were tender and pink, covered in sparse puffs of down that somehow made them look more naked. Now, on their twelfth day of living, their skin is black and pricked with feathers. Their mother is no longer the sole trigger for their fits of energy. Sometimes, when she is away, they cheep and fidget in the nest. "Where are you?" they cry. "And why have you abandoned us?" This is an evolution. They don't just come alive to eat; they come alive remembering they want to live.

Another milestone: the cessation of the fecal sac. Instead, in their burgeoning maturity, they push their butts over the edge of the nest and streak the side of the apartment building with greyish, gluey shit. I eat my peanut butter toast and ponder this development. Are they hinting at my own next evolution? No more garbage bag for Robbie to collect. I'll toss my newest acquisitions out the window: a decal declaring my support for NPR, a drywall hammer, a candle-making kit, shoe polish, a pink beret, and Boggle. I imagine all the lettered dice lying in the parking lot. But if a word forms with no one to read it, is it really there?

The mother bird isn't bothered by her babies' stream of shit, but my south-facing neighbors are not so easygoing. Maybe they'll call Robbie and tell him that I've lost my mind. Then he'll appear below my window with a garbage bag and a grabby claw. I'll be wearing my cutest clothes, including the push up bra that I haven't yet discarded, and I'll lean out the window and dazzle Robbie with my verbal virtuosity. I'll crack jokes and stun him with the power of my metaphors. I'll make deep observations into the state of the world. I live on the third floor, which is close enough to ground level that he should be able to hear me if I shout really loud through the mask.

Robbie never stood out to me in normal life. He was neither particularly handsome nor particularly gross. He didn't leer at me like the previous maintenance man, but he also couldn't perform MacGyver-type repairs like fixing my leaky sink with a tube sock and a stick of gum. In fact, he made the problem worse and then got soaked and had to call the plumber. But all that doesn't matter anymore. He is a passable human; so am I. He has a body; so do I. My brief time with the stranger never satisfies my hunger. It only makes me hungrier. It turns each of my pores into a tiny, starving mouth, begging for contact with so much desperation that the fear recedes.

"Robbie," I murmur to myself at night, when the mother and the father swallow are perched on the edge of the nest with their heads tucked beneath their wings and all their progeny are spread out before them, silent and still. But I don't fantasize about having sex with Robbie, I just imagine spooning him in bed. I don't even care which spoon I am, though I used to emphasize on dating profiles that I was only interested in Small Spoon duties. Now all I want is a body next to mine.

Two days ago, I tossed two objects out my window. The pink beret frisbeed a great distance. The shoe polish fell straight down and smashed itself into a ring of pigment. Alongside the body of the bird that died, they form a strange tableau. I wait and wait, but Robbie never comes. Maybe quarantine has made my neighbors more accepting. Maybe they're not even there. Before the plague arrived, the couple on my left had loud sex on a creaky bed, the degenerate on my right blasted Nickelback, and the grandchildren of the woman down the hall ran noisily up the stairs on Sunday mornings. Now all I hear is the impatient cheeping of the baby birds.

"It was a bad plan to begin with," says Ariel.

"Throw something else," suggests Mary.

Now they bicker all the time. Only the stranger can silence them, but the stranger grows less effective every day. My body has adapted—numb or not, it knows that hand is mine. I slap myself. It has less sting. I tickle myself on the sensitive spot at the back of my knees, but no longer do I feel the need to laugh. I caress myself—it is my own dull hand, so familiar that it hardly has the strength to stir sensation. When I push the sequence of moles on my body, my body does not open or respond.

I go to my corkboard and take down the business card with Robbie's cell, but when I dial the number I'm confronted by an automated voice.

"I'm sorry," says the brusque robot lady from Verizon. "The mailbox is full and cannot accept a message at this time. Please try again later. Goodbye."

I pace down the long hall in my apartment. I use it for exercise, though before the plague I labeled it a waste of space. I ponder the babies. Today is their sixteenth day of living. They've developed rust-colored feathers on their breasts that make them look like honest-to-God swallows. They're fascinated by the things I've thrown—they perch on the edge of the nest and squawk frantically at the pink beret, ruffling their feathers, flapping their wings.

"I think you should prepare yourself—"Ariel begins, but Mary cuts her off.

"Are you over sixty-two and worried that you won't be able to maintain your quality of life?" asks Mary. "If so, a reverse mortgage may be right for you."

Dutifully, I sit down and take dictation.

I inform my mother that the world is full of horrors.

"Yes," she says. "I know."

According to Audubon Online, these include declining insect populations, habitat loss, cold spells, climate change, avian lice, predatory bats, cats, and pesticides.

"Mariel, are you okay?" my mother asks.

"I'm outraged," I answer. "They're just gonna let their babies throw themselves out of the nest."

"It's a natural part of parenting."

"But is that sweet?"

"Of course it is," she answers. "If you care about your children, you let them go, even when the world is all fucked up. Like when I dropped you off at college. Remember that? I put on a brave face when I was helping you move, but afterwards I parked around the block and sobbed. I didn't want you to know. I wanted you to feel it was okay to go."

"But now I'm trapped in this apartment and I can't come home."

"This too shall pass," she says, but it's only her optimism speaking, and I know it isn't true.

Twenty days after the hatching of the eggs, I get out of bed and find one baby left. Then I fall to my knees and keen.

"No, no, no," I cry.

The baby cocks its head with quick jerky movements that make it look like it's assessing the situation. But it can't assess anything, because its brain is the size of a lentil. It alternates between peering over the edge of the nest and snapping its beak back in a frenzy of grooming. When it stretches out its sharp gray wing to search for mites, I am amazed. It's like inspecting a newborn's hand and realizing that all the bits and parts and joints are there. Its wing is longer than its body, perfectly feathered, perfectly formed. The baby looks like a plumper, softer version of its parents. Rust-colored feathers fuzz out around its breast.

"Don't leave," I beg.

"Call your mother," says Ariel. "You know what she'll tell you to do."

"But your phone's too far away," purrs Mary. "Turn your back for one second and the last baby'll leave the nest. And you know what that means—"

Ariel answers with the steady cadence of a well-learned list.

"It grows up. It finds a mate. It builds a nest. Another clutch of eggs. The world goes on."

"No." Mary savors the negation. "It means the parents leave. Momma and Poppa Swallow. Abandon the nest. Abandon the baby. Whaddya think? Maybe it'll live another week before it smashes itself into a window or gets exposed to some extra toxic pesticide. Then one of its wings won't work and it will drag itself through the dirt until a cat shows up to play a little game."

"Appealing to fear," says Ariel. "It can drive sales, but it won't build long-term brand loyalty."

The baby returns to the edge of the nest. Opens its wings. Chirps frantically. Closes them again. Its breast has the perfect roundness of a Christmas bauble.

"Are you stuck at home alone?" muses Mary. "Wondering what gives meaning to your life. No kids? No pets? Ant farm doesn't do it for ya? Can't cuddle a sea monkey? If you're looking for comfort in these unprecedented times, take action today. The future is within your reach."

The baby gazes at the world with such dumb longing. It doesn't understand there's nothing there—there is only this apartment here, the three of us: Mary, Ariel, and me. I open the window. I fold my hand around the baby's body. It's so used to me that it doesn't even flinch. It is very light, very living. According to Audubon Online, a barn swallow weighs the same as three sheets of paper or half a slice of wholegrain bread.

"We'll take care of you forever," I say.

Alphabet

amanda laughtland

I'll draw a rebus by hand
or use pictures from magazines
or stickers from the dollar store
of rainbows and wild animals
or photos I take with my phone
where I smile instead of pretending
to be remotely badass
as I cut away every word
and most letters to make
a skeleton key for any lock
that keeps you from finding me.

Shows Light Wear

alice lowe

I feel a kinship with readers who leave their marks, like calling cards, in the margins of used books. Like when you meet a stranger's eyes reaching for the same bottle of wine off a shelf and acknowledge your shared inclinations: "I love this with pizza, don't you?" I trace the telltale footprints, intuit what their owners deemed important or inspiring or confounding, what they liked or didn't like.

Several years ago, I bought a paperback copy of A. S. Byatt's *Angels and Insects* at a neighborhood used bookstore. The pages were peppered with underlined words, starred passages, cursory notes. The signs of rigorous activity told me that its previous owner was a student, stumbling through unfamiliar terrain. I like to imagine him, midway through the book, becoming swept up by the twisting tale, enamored with the lyrical language.

Byatt isn't easy reading. Her prose demonstrates sophisticated thought; her vocabulary is challenging. My predecessor may have underlined unfamiliar words that he intended to look up. Or perhaps he liked Byatt's eclectic word choices. Fifty-four underlined words in fifty pages (omitting duplications and foreign words in italics), include: *amorphous, abeyance, assiduously, citron, coppice, carapace, didactic, draconian,* and *depredation.* Also, *roundel, midge, complaisance, viscous, higgledy-piggledy, inimical, orcs, formicary, interstices, perforce, pullulation, parthenogenesis, smutched, sanguine,* and *sagacity.* Others are terms for fabrics—*gauze, tulle, organdie, calico, muslin, damask*—which lead to my arguable assumption of the masculine pronoun: when my husband is at a loss for a word in a crossword puzzle, it's often some kind of yard goods.

The asterisks are more perplexing. One to four stars are interposed above selected words and phrases: "he had written a daily examination of his conscience" – one star; "whose flames flickered" – two stars; "a simple row of pearls, soft white" – three stars; "he felt dirty and dangerous" – four stars. With no common thread running through them, I'm clueless as to what the ciphers might signify. I chalk it up to the bifurcated nature of book markings. They're private, readers' notes to themselves, but they become public when the book changes hands.

Poet Billy Collins shares my fascination with books' previous readers. In "Marginalia," he observes that some notes are fierce "skirmishes against the author," while others are offhand responses like "Please!" and "Ha!" Check marks and exclamation points that, "rain down along the sidelines" are added by "fans who cheer from the empty bleachers." He asserts that we've all done it, "seized the white perimeter as our own / and reached for a pen...." No, not all. Some people insist vehemently they would never deface a book. They're dismayed by others' seeming lack of respect, judging it on a continuum from slight annoyance to criminal vandalism.

I have a writer friend in that camp. Recently she sent me a marked copy of a story collection she liked. Notations in the book were clearly those of a writer: a line drawn under the penultimate paragraph of a story, with the comment, "This is where it should end," a box drawn around every use of the word "like"—I agreed it was excessive—with an asterisk in the margin. I told my friend I appreciated her annotations, and she replied, "NOT MY NOTES!! I would never write in a book."

I had a roommate in the seventies whose politics skewed to the extreme right. She gave me a copy of her favorite book, *Atlas Shrugged*, by Ayn Rand. "You *have* to read it," she said. The book was a new hardback that she had gone through page by page with a yellow highlighter, scoring significant passages. She neither converted me to her libertarian views nor created a rift in our friendship—I accepted her gift as well intended. My motivations were pure when I bought a copy of Erica Jong's *Fear of Fifty* for another friend when she reached that milestone age. I knew she'd appreciate Jong's wry and witty take on the mid-life passage, but my friend abhorred the "F-word." She never said it and was affronted when others did. *Fear of Fifty* was awash with the offending four-letter bomb, so before gift-wrapping it I went through with a black Sharpie and blotted out every fuck.

For the past thirty years I've studied and written about the life and work of Virginia Woolf, so my Woolf books are heavily notated. Two copies each of *A Writer's Diary* and *A Room of One's Own* are crammed with Post-its, the endpapers black and blue with penned notations, the pages annotated and highlighted in different colors for different research projects. They spring to life as I scan my notes: papers I wrote on Woolf and food, Woolf's self-writing, her use of repetition and color, her relationships with other writers.

My copy of *Jacob's Room* came stamped in perpetuity with another's identity. "David Sanchez '90" is printed in block capital letters on the fore edges, top, bottom, and side. In the margins David—I feel we're on a first-name basis—parsed Jacob's character with bracketed passages and notes of description and interpretation ("Jacob likes life at Cambridge." "Sandra has him hooked.") He noted personal traits, time passages, location shifts, curiosities. When David came to the mention of a Moorish kiosk, he could have breezed past it, but to his credit he researched it. Written over the words is "band stand," and in the margin is a line drawing identified as a kiosk, Moorish-looking at that. Years after adding my own notes I still can differentiate them—straighter and lighter, thin blue pen or gray pencil lines—from David's gashes of black ink.

I volunteer an afternoon a week at Bluestocking Books, the lone holdout on a block that once housed several used bookstores. Kris, the owner, just celebrated her store's twentieth anniversary, but the site has housed a bookstore for more than fifty years. Bluestocking seems like a fixture in the neighborhood but staffing and resources are spread thin. I believe books should be a renewable resource; my small contribution may help to assure the shop's continuity and save some books from the landfill.

I enter books donated or received on trade into the database, then onto the shelves. More than half of the books Kris takes in have some kind of marking in them. She gives them a new lease on life whenever possible, rejecting only those beyond redemption. In accordance with industry standards, I note each book's condition, designate most of them good to very good-plus, listing details: writing in margins, creased pages, often falling back on the catch-all "shows light wear." A bottom-level category of acceptable promises only that the book is readable, its pages and cover intact. At first, I was too generous with my rankings—my fondness for lived-in books blinded me to flaws that others might find objectionable. I've learned to squelch my penchant for personalization and assess them more critically.

Mortimer Adler, the author of *How to Read a Book*, defends marking in books as an act of love rather than mutilation. We own a book, he says, not just by buying it but by absorbing it into our bloodstream. I open a book with a pencil or highlighter at hand. A clever choice of words, a perfect metaphor, an evocative description—I underscore or bracket them, place an asterisk in the margin, jot down a word or two. Marking books helps me remember what I read, imprint it on my brain, and find it again. I don't say, "I wish I'd written this," but that's what might sometimes be read between the lines, literally, in my cryptic symbols. I flag pages with stickers and scraps so I can go back and transfer my notes to the endpapers or to my writing notebook.

I flip through the pages of a beloved novel, *The Lost Garden* by Helen Humphreys. It's full of notes and references, as I've read it several times and written an essay about its homage to Virginia Woolf. I stop at a lightly underlined passage: "I am thinking now that I much prefer parsnips to people. They are infinitely more reliable." The narrator, a horticulturalist, is a loner, uncomfortable with people, unsure of herself in social situations. That penciled line translates as: "Mm, yeah, I've been there." Another, "I could thread myself through London moving from leafy square to leafy square," evokes my latent Anglophilia, the years I was swept up in the aura of London's tree-shaded parks and neighborhoods. I don't need words; the emphasis is enough to stir my memory.

I don't think about who will read my notes and what they'll think when, in periodic purges to free up limited shelf space, I pull down books to donate to Bluestocking, my local library branch, or one of the rapidly proliferating Little Free Libraries. I leaf through them and pause at my markings and margin notes. It's like reading old diaries, picking up past conversations with myself. Sometimes my notes will induce me to keep a book—an interesting reference, a memory elicited, a gorgeous sentence. This book meant something to me; I may want to read it again. I send the discards on to find their next owners. Who might wonder why I underlined a particular passage; what my asterisks and exclamations mean. Who might respond to my notes and feel a kinship with me, nod and say, "I love this sentence too."

fiction

Longer Boats
max talley

Grant Peterson felt summer dying all around him that Friday. Just La-bor Day weekend until school began. The rest of the year a slog of numbers, dates, and reading assignments.

"Grant," his mother said during the ferry ride to Nantucket Island, "apparently, there's only one room left at our hotel." She gently touched her sprayed, upswept hair that looked ready to launch from her head. "So, you'll stay at Uncle Raymond's."

Raymond wasn't Grant's uncle. More a godfather. But Raymond's two daughters, age fifteen and sixteen, regarded Grant as a boy hobbled with being a mere thirteen. They were tall and developed, and gossiped and dreamed of high school seniors, or really old guys in college.

"We'll meet you for lunch," his mother continued, "or possibly dinner."

On the outer decks, large American flags whipped in the breeze, ac-knowledging the Bicentennial. 1976 signified just another year to Grant.

Rolling off the ferry ramp, Grant's father drove their rented AMC Pac-er west on Madaket Road. He yawed north on Eel Point Road to Uncle Raymond's cottage: a cedar-shingled, unpainted wood structure turned gray from the stormy coastal winters. Unlike the historic homes down-town, it was a sprawling single-story house perched on a cliff. A wood-en walkway that became a stairway descended over the rise and through dunes to the beach.

Grant's father pumped his friend's hand outside. "See you and Sandra tomorrow." Raymond had divorced and now dated Sandra Wallace, a close friend of Grant's parents.

A rumble of ignition and a belch of exhaust left Grant alone.

Inside, a central living room connected to a kitchen area where two cor-ridors snaked off toward bedrooms. Raymond's daughters stood waiting, as if summoned to a military tribunal.

"Isabel, Amanda," Raymond said. "You remember Grant. He'll be stay-ing in the guest room." He pointed down one hallway.

The girls flashed pained smiles and blinked, revealing matching light blue eye shadow. They retreated through sliding doors out to the deck.

"Don't mind them," Raymond said. "If I didn't have a beach house, they'd be with their mother this summer." He sighed. "I'm off to dinner.

Sandwiches are in the fridge, okay?"

The girls soon clomped out on dates, Isabel wearing platforms, Amanda in pumps.

Grant watched *The Rockford Files* as he rifled through record crates. Uncle Raymond was near fifty, but dressed in faded jeans and Earth Shoes, and plastered his living room with posters: Nixon sporting only a Watergate Hotel towel around his waist, The Eagles, bearded and glowering, and Jimmy Carter smiling and youthful.

After reading three chapters of *Cat's Cradle*, Grant fell asleep.

He woke hearing Raymond strumming a guitar. "I didn't know you played," Grant said, joining him in the morning-lit living room.

"The girls biked to town so it's safe." Raymond laughed. "Your mother called. Said they were too busy to have lunch. But they'll see you on the drive home."

"Oh..."

"Any plans today?"

"Check out the beach," Grant said, "maybe swim."

Raymond squinted. "Don't swim alone, okay? The neighbor kids are friendly enough."

Around 11:30, Grant descended the wooden stairway through the long strands of beach grass and sparse stunted trees. He wore a short-sleeved, button-down shirt over Hawaiian trunks that hung to his knees. In a small knapsack, he crammed his Kurt Vonnegut paperback, a cap, cassette tapes, Coppertone lotion, and a Saran-wrapped ham and Kraft cheese sandwich.

Grant only traveled two hundred yards before encountering three boys bunched by the surf. The biggest, maybe fourteen, the others about twelve.

The tall one turned. "Who are you? Where you from?"

"Grant." He pointed behind. "Visiting my Uncle Raymond."

The boy relaxed. "I'm Kevin. Look what we found." A two-foot dead fish lay on its side among wet purple kelp, one large round eye gazing upward. "It's a sea bass." Kevin poked at it with a stick. "I told George and Marcus we're going to gut it. Maybe find something valuable inside."

The air smelled of rank seaweed, low tide, and sunbaked decaying things.

Kevin pulled a serrated knife from a vinyl bag. "Marcus? George?"

Marcus shook his head.

George appeared nauseous.

"Cowards." Kevin slid the fish over to a sand cliff carved out by the night tide. Then sitting, he sliced into the fish's belly. The viscous guts spilled out over his hands and onto the beach to be haloed by flies.

George bent over and vomited.

Marcus looked away and so did Grant—avoiding the Domino Effect.

"You want to hang around with us?" Kevin brandished the oozing fish by its tail. "Well, help out."

"That's okay."

Kevin offered Grant his knife. "Dig deep to see if it swallowed any coins."

If Grant refused, they would shun him, the weekend stretching to eternity as he sulked by Raymond's stairway.

"Come on," Marcus said.

"Take the knife," Kevin told Grant. "What, are you chicken?"

She arrived with quiet precision, padding over on sandals. A little bit older, fourteen or fifteen, Grant thought. A white button-down shirt tied above the waist exposed her belly button, while the faded blue jean shorts below were cut ragged.

The girl moved with confidence in between the boys and stared at Grant. "Come with me." She walked west.

Grant looked at Kevin's anxious face, the grotesque fish, and then toward the girl's retreating figure. He followed.

"Where you going?" Kevin said. "Stay away from her. She's wicked weird."

Grant ignored his words and caught up with her stride.

"Those guys are stupid," she said. "You don't belong with them." She stopped to drink in Grant's features. "Wait, how old are you? What's your name?"

"Grant." He felt his mouth twist. The gig was up. "Thirteen." His cheeks burned and he'd only just come outside.

"Oh," she said, "I thought you were much older, like fourteen." She had dirty blonde hair, the front chin-length and gusting about her face, the rest tied in a braid descending her back.

"Fourteen in December," Grant said and she smiled. He felt better. She didn't act like girls in his grade, calling Grant stupid or mocking him. "What's your name?"

"Analisa," she replied. "Can I look through your knapsack?" She had already slipped it off his shoulder.

"Anna or Lisa?"

"Neither, silly. Both." She laughed, but it wasn't jeering, more of an isn't-everything-funny-and-strange laugh.

"Keep up with me." Analisa strolled on the soft damp sand as she examined his possessions. The foamy slap of waves wet their feet before sounding a carbonated fizz of retreat. Seagulls shrieked while circling above, and piping plovers and willets pecked along the shoreline for food.

"Walk like we're friends." She gripped Grant's shirt-sleeve and pulled him toward her, then let go, using both hands to rummage through his knapsack.

Up close, Analisa smelled of sun-warmed skin, sea salt, coconut tanning lotion, and unwashed hair.

"*Cat's Cradle.* Is that a good book, Grant?"

"I think it is."

"My mother read *Breakfast of Champions* but wouldn't let me because of the dirty pictures. So, I snuck in her room when she was out and looked."

"Were there?"

"Yup. Drawings of pubic hair and you know, body parts." She paused, the surf frothing her ankles, and gave him a sidelong glance. "You've taken biology, right?"

"Yeah, sure," Grant lied. Sex-Ed would be taught during fall by Sheldon Roller, PE coach and sometime science teacher. A bear of a man with a crewcut. He advised the boys during recess, "You're most important investment is a supporter—a jockstrap. Underwear gives no protection."

"Look what I brought." Analisa removed a fire engine red, plastic Panasonic tape player with a black wristband from her carry bag. She moved to the dry sand and plunked down on her haunches, crossing her legs.

Grant followed and crouched, neither sitting nor standing.

She reviewed his cassettes. "Grand Funk? No. Bad Company? No. Kiss?" She paused. "Can I bury this one and we'll both forget you ever had it?"

"Okay."

"No, it's not okay, Grant," Analisa said. "Stick up for what you like." She returned his knapsack and lifted a cassette from her own bag. "Do you know *Tea for the Tillerman*?"

"Cat Stevens."

"You think he's just for girls, right?"

"No, my cousins like him. They're guys."

"Sit here." She tapped the sand by her side. "You look really awkward." He collapsed and scooted over.

"*Longer Boats* is my favorite." Analisa pressed the play button and acoustic guitar sounded, followed by Cat Steven's velvety rasp. She unfurled her towel and lay back, then started singing along.

The song seemed to capture the moment, the rhythm matching the lapping waves, coastal noises on the tape blending with avian cries overhead. Grant sat bunched up, gripping his knees. Staring northwest beyond the kids lolling in the shallows, he watched the lazy procession of one ferry approaching Nantucket Harbor, another departing.

Grant angled his neck. He could see through Analisa's white shirt to the crocheted blue bikini-top underneath. She wasn't top-heavy like Debbie Steinberg from his class, who seemed to have transformed to a woman at thirteen.

"What are you doing?" She slid the mirrored sunglasses down her nose.

"Nothing, I was listening..."

Analisa burst out laughing and kicked sand at him. "Staring is rude." She pulled off her shirt, slid out of her cut-offs, and flipped over on her stomach. "Rub some lotion on my back. It's in the bag."

Grant squirted the cool cream onto her warm skin and she flinched. He lightly massaged her shoulders.

"I'm not delicate," she said. "Rub harder."

Grant did, gazing down at her tanned back, only broken by the bikini top's thin straps.

"You're not going to do anything weird, are you?"

"What?"

"You know, try to steal my top, so I have to get up to grab it?"

"No. Has that happened?"

Analisa lay her head on its side. "You seem different." Her forehead was furrowed with thought.

Grant suddenly felt self-conscious straddled above her. He swung his leg over to sit two feet away, facing out toward the swell of the sea.

Families trudged by. Bickering parents carried beach umbrellas and baskets as children of various sizes trailed them, shadowed beneath drooping hats. The afternoon sun made everything drowsy under its bleaching glare. The day itself slouching to a halt from heat exhaustion. Even gulls had given up flying to watch the dapple of light on waves while perched along the shoreline.

"Where do you live, Analisa?"

She propped herself up on her elbows and pointed east. "Toward Jetties Beach. In a dingy old house with a screened-in porch. It's embarrassing."

Grant nodded.

"We should keep walking." Analisa scooped up a handful of sand, letting the grains slip through her fingers. "This is all we have left of summer."

She stared at Grant, and he basked under her green-eyed gaze—neither worshipful nor judgmental, but accepting. He lived in splendor for that prolonged moment and imagined her radiating glow finally burning off the fog of childhood's lingering dream.

Analisa buttoned the white shirt that draped down to her thighs, pressed her shorts into the carry bag, and stood. "You take the tape player."

They continued eastward, only pausing to watch an old man fishing from the shore. His face appeared as weathered and pitted as the pilings on the harbor docks.

"Catch anything?" Analisa asked.

"A small bluefish." The old man frowned. "A striped bass broke my line." His eyes goggled at Analisa's legs, then he turned to concentrate on the sea.

"Let's go to the point and watch the ferries coming in," Analisa told Grant. "We'll have a picnic. Did you bring any food?"

"You know I did."

She punched his shoulder gently. "We can split your sandwich."

They slogged onward beneath the dazzle of mid-afternoon sunlight, veering toward the damp sand where the tread was easier. Grant walked ahead.

"Look out." Analisa pulled him back against her. "Horseshoe crab." A spiny tail protruded upwards where the prehistoric-looking crustacean had buried itself. "They can puncture your foot."

Grant felt her pressed close and a quivery electric spark tickled through him. He pulled away. "Thanks." Grant thought a moment. "Do you stay out here year-round?"

"No, just for the summer." She gestured toward Hyannis, or Cape Cod, or the continent itself. They continued, stepping over driftwood and sand-dusted towels.

"Hey, watch it," a girl of perhaps sixteen yelled. "We're in the middle of a game." A group of bronzed girls in matching bathing suits played volleyball, their court apparently extending to the shoreline.

Grant and Analisa detoured knee-deep into the water. Varsity status and trophy cups had given these players the hard, arrogant faces of grownups. Their last weekend of summer and they sure as hell were going to enjoy every single moment of fun they were entitled to.

"Ow." Analisa's face contorted. "A jellyfish."

Grant led her ashore. A red welt rose on her shin. He noticed her eyes watering, but she pulled up a shirt tail and wiped them dry.

"I'm not like most girls," she said. "I don't cry. But shit, that really stings."

They had reached a deserted area between Dionis Beach and Jetties Beach. The joyous screams of children and scolding voices of parents receded behind them. Scalloped cirrus clouds formed a canopy above, as if the land and sea had conspired with the sky to cool the sun's glare.

Grant brought Analisa, her arm anchored around his shoulder, toward two abandoned beach chairs. Their aluminum frames showed rust and worn plastic fabric strips. While she sat massaging her shin, Grant divided the sandwich using his Swiss Army Knife. He handed her the larger half. The ham tasted warm and moist, the cheese bland, and the Wonder Bread had hardened, but it was the best thing he'd ever eaten.

Grant studied the beach. Brittle husks of black skate shells waited to be wave-battered, pummeled into dried bits that would pepper the salt-glazed sand. Long tangles of shiny greenish kelp extended like intestines of leviathans from the deep. Purple-black seaweed embraced a dented buoy next to cracked clam shells, discarded bottles, starfish—presumably dead, but who could tell?—blue soft glass, and dozens of sea-smoothed stones.

Analisa examined one. "Do you think these came from outer space? Like chunks of meteors?"

"Don't know," Grant replied. "But that sounds cool."

"Not too much further." She lifted Grant from the low-slung chair.

"Did we pass your house?"

"Ages ago. I told you, it's a mess. We're not going there."

"Just wanted to know where you lived."

"So you could visit me at midnight?" She pinched him.

Two older boys approached from the east. Grant tried to steer Analisa around them, but they shifted to meet head on.

The bigger guy walked straight up to Analisa. "Is that your boyfriend? Or just for today?"

"He's my friend," she said. "As if it's any business of yours."

"I liked you last summer. Remember? You split."

"I don't remember you—at all." Analisa frowned.

"Because you're a tease. A bitch."

"Don't call her that," Grant said.

"Says who?" the burly guy replied. "What are you, twelve?"

Behind him, the smaller boy dangled a horseshoe crab by the tail and slammed its shell down on the hard sand.

"I think you should show us your boobs," the big guy said to Analisa, leering.

"Yeah," added his friend.

"You owe me." The leader tugged at her shirt collar.

Grant bent his head down and rushed forward, ramming the guy's stomach.

"You little bastard." He doubled over, gasping. Straightening himself, he punched Grant in the jaw and again just above the eye. Grant landed on his back. He got up dizzy, but crouched, preparing to charge again.

"Are you crazy?" The big guy held his belly. "I'll kick your ass, and she's not even worth it." He edged closer; hands bunched into fists.

Analisa swung the Panasonic player, striking the boy's forehead, and he staggered for an instant. Grant kicked his shin, hobbling him, before Analisa cracked the tape player hard against his skull. The guy stumbled and fell sideways into the shallows, gripping his head. Using both hands, he pushed himself to his knees, his face monstrous with pain.

"We're going to kill both of you..." he started to say, then saw his friend sprinting west along the shoreline, "...tomorrow."

Analisa took Grant's arm and they ran east until both crumpled onto the sand, exhausted. She laughed in gasps and pressed her cheek against his sore jaw.

"I'm sorry. I couldn't protect you."

"You tried," she said. "Besides, he was older." The damaged tape player dangled in her grip. Analisa sighed. "I ruined my Cat Stevens cassette." She extracted it, the tape unspooling and tangled. "But we showed that bully."

"I can buy you a new tape tomorrow."

She stared off at the horizon. "Yeah...tomorrow."

"What time is it?"

"Nearly six," she said. "Let's rest before heading home."

Grant was too dazed to argue.

Analisa unrolled the beach towel in the dunes so they could lay down out of sight. She removed her shirt to use as a blanket when they snuggled together. "I didn't think it would be you today."

"What?"

She placed Grant's right hand on her left breast. "Ow. Softer." Analisa slid her fingers under his shirt to delicately stroke his chest. "Like that."

He followed her directions until she giggled and said, "Stop."

"Was that wrong?"

"No." She pressed her legs against Grant. "We'll kiss later." Analisa hugged him, her breathing heavy. Wind buffeted the sand dunes, the long beach grass hissing at the assault then whispering as the air calmed.

Grant realized Analisa had fallen asleep so he shut his eyes too.

He woke up shivering, the last embers of sunset dying to the west. Grant squinted in every direction, but Analisa and her towel were gone. Only the broken Panasonic lodged in the sand convinced him the day had been real. The beacon from Brant Point Lighthouse arced through the darkness. Colored lights drifted away from the harbor—a retreating ferry—but it signified nothing. Grant stood, shook his head to clear his thoughts, and followed the lit-up beach house windows back east.

Uncle Raymond waited with a flashlight at the foot of his steps. "Jesus Christ, I thought you'd drowned." They mounted the wooden stairway together into an explosion of light inside.

"Where the hell were you?" Raymond asked, his expression a blend of anger and concern. "It's almost nine. Your face. What happened?"

"I met a girl."

Raymond's daughters peeked out from the hallway and laughed.

"And she hit you?"

"No, I protected her from an older boy."

The redness drained from Raymond's complexion. "That's wild," he said, half-smiling. "I'll get some ice. Let's hope the swelling goes away by Monday so your folks don't freak out."

"You're not going to tell?"

"Hell, no," he said. "No one's going to." Raymond eyed his daughters. "Right?"

They stamped back to their room.

After a late dinner, Grant dozed off listening to the concussion of waves against the shore.

On Sunday morning, Grant put on a tennis hat to hide his bruise and tramped down the beach searching. Girls sprouted everywhere, but not Analisa.

He finally found the weather-beaten house with a long screened-in porch up on a bluff. Climbing through the dunes, Grant pressed his face against the screen. It smelled like ointment and powdery perfume, of dust and dryness, of old people. A bloated cat lazed on a rocking chair.

"Hello?" Grant rapped his knuckles against the wood of the screen door until a woman older than his grandmother shuffled over in a bathrobe and slippers.

"What is it?" She squeaked the door open. "Are you the paper boy?"

"No, is your, uh, granddaughter here, Analisa?"

"Analisa?" she said. "There are no children here. Go play somewhere else." She slapped the door shut.

Grant tried the neighboring houses without luck, a jagged panic lancing his stomach. He meandered along the beach before encountering the boys with the dead fish.

"Did your girlfriend ditch you?" Kevin asked.

"No," Grant said. "I can't find Analisa. Do you know which house she lives in?"

Kevin stopped tossing the Frisbee to his friends. "That girl doesn't live here. She takes the ferry from Hyannis on weekends, causes trouble for a day, then goes home." He gave Grant an incredulous look. "I tried to warn you. Most local guys know to stay away." He twirled his orange Frisbee. "I doubt she'll be back. Maybe next June." The boy who disemboweled a fish yesterday, now acted almost tender. "She leads guys on then disappears. They wander around dazed for the rest of the summer." His mouth tightened. "You got lucky. Because summer's over tomorrow."

Grant spent much of Sunday languishing on the planks of a jetty, watching ancient fishermen cast their lines as the ferries came and went. Still only thirteen and he already felt old, like the broken and discarded Panasonic tape player.

Grant returned to Raymond's at four and they walked the cobblestone streets of town where he purchased a copy of *Tea for the Tillerman.*

Cat Stevens became the soundtrack of that fall and following spring, but eventually he forgot about the album, forgot about Analisa.

***

In Whole Foods forty years later, Grant waited at the brightly-lit bar while his wife bought gluten-free zucchini bread. When "Longer Boats" played, the entire weekend came back to him. But Uncle Raymond was dead now, home prices on Nantucket even higher than in the Hamptons, Cat Stevens had become Yusef Islam, and no one like Jimmy Carter would ever be President again.

Grant closed his eyes to summon a final memory.

Before they fell asleep huddled together that beach Saturday in the shadows of late afternoon, Analisa had pointed at a sluggish, confused house fly.

"If you could live for just one day, Grant, would this be that day?"

"Maybe. I guess. I don't know."

She squeezed his arm. "It would be for me..."

Grant opened his eyes.

A woman seated nearby at the Whole Foods bar looked over. "This song always gets to me too." She handed him a napkin, smiled, then turned back to drink her red wine.

A few obscene words escape

timothy pilgrim

my mouth, not to mention,
                        a wounded sparrow of despair
        flying out of my soul
                as I watch her drive away,
                        the whole thermos of mimosas
        nestled between her thighs,
                warm brioche with cherry filling
lying on the seat beside.

French Class

kirby wright

The class was split in half, with two rows of chairs facing each other. Miss Davies, a heavyset teacher in a tailored blue muumuu, rambled on in Parisian behind a podium fronting the chalkboard. Speaking English was *interdit*. Students were to keep their eyes on Miss Davies.

The boy gazed across the room at the girl opposite him, the one with the aqua skirt. Her blonde hair spilled past her shoulders. Sometimes she tucked the errant strands behind her ears to keep them in place. She wore a necklace of irregular puka shells resembling jagged teeth. Her beauty mark reminded him of Marilyn Monroe. She stretched her brown legs teasing him to touch her. Her hair was streaked green. He knew that was from the Punahou pool, where she practiced synchronized swimming. He smelled chlorine whenever she passed. The boy had felt like a creature obsessed, sneaking past the gym and squinting through the cyclone fence protecting the pool. He'd watched her lift a leg high out of the water, arch the foot, and stick toes into the sun.

His days were meha and dark before he'd seen her. He'd always sing along to "Ma Belle Amie" on his transistor and tried imagining a girl-friend. Now the belle amie had arrived. It felt as if his life hung in the balance, but he was overwhelmed by a fear of losing her. He wondered if fear might tip her away. But was he worthy? He despised his dark complexion, his average build, and his slanted eyes. He wished for a magic lever to pull so he could swing her into his arms. He imagined them being stranded on a deserted island and holding her tight in the shallows while the Trades toyed her hair.

The girl tapped a slipper on the tiles. She pursed her lips. Was she humming? The boy pretended to be on a Parisian street. "*Bonjour, mademoiselle,*" he whispered, "*je t'aime.*" She met his eyes and offered a sly smile. It was the kind of smile that forced him to look away because it burned her image into his soul. His heart rocked on earthquake ground. Had she heard him or read his lips? God, she was still smiling. His skin trembled as he struggled for a foothold on earth quivering with desire.

Miss Davies stood at a table beside the podium. Her brown-edged table was waffle-thin. A slide projector and a record player were perched on top. A classmate turned off the overhead fluorescents. Davies pressed a clicker—a circular tray of slides perked to life. She placed a needle on the spinning record and the silver screen against the far wall flashed cartoon images of a couple. Davies advanced the slides to match the record's narration: Monsieur and Madame Thibaut lived by the Eiffel Tower and shopped at the boulangerie. They bought baguettes, espresso, and steaks with fries. The boy saw himself as Monsieur Thibaut and the girl as his wife. They lived in an alternate universe where they spent their days strolling the banks of the Seine.

The boy looked away from the screen. His eyes met the girl's in the half-light. This time he didn't look away. He recognized a longing in her that mirrored his own, a hunger to be held. Her lips parted. Here was the acknowledgment he'd craved, a communion that made him feel wanted. A switch kicked on inside him, turning his world into a bright place.

The needle slashed across the record. The screen froze. There was a scene of the Thibauts entertaining guests in their flat. The fluorescents came on, causing the boy to shield his eyes with a hand. Miss Davies ambled down the aisle between rows and stopped in front of him. She crossed her fleshy arms. "Monsieur?" she asked.

"Oui, Madame Davies?"

"Prenes vos yeux de la jeune fille."

The boy recognized "yeux" and" "jeune fille" and married the words. His classmates chuckled.

The bell sounded. Miss Davies reminded the students to check their schedules for their next assignment. The girl glided by the boy flashing her sly smile. She vanished out the door. But she'd found passage to his secret place of longing. He realized that, no matter what happened in the world beyond French class, the girl would be a part of him until the day he died.

Weather for Samantha K

paul curley

The Kims call the messiahs tattletales and whiny bitches. Let's add lucky fucks. Messiah Max stops me in the hall to complain that they're *doing it again* in the men's shower. I've got a briefing on the wildfire in five minutes, but I detour to the South Wing.

"Knock, knock, everybody dressed?" I call out before I enter. Butterflies in the stomach, hoping it's not Samantha K. As I step inside, the resident scents of mold and menthol mingle with interloper lavender. Sure enough, my favorite Kim is buttoning her blouse in the mirror over the sink. Her hair is dripping, causing a wet patch to spread across her back.

The shower is still running. I peek around the corner to find Messiah Jack kneeling ass naked on the tiles, prayer fists squeezed so tight in front of his face that his knuckles have turned dice white. "God forgive me. Please God, please God," he says. He just took a shower with a beautiful woman. He should be *thanking* God. I kill the shower, but his pleas for mercy will keep wasting like water down the drain unless I snap him out of it.

"For Christ's sake, Jack, get some clothes on," I say.

Hands on the tiles, he pushes himself to standing and points at me. "Don't. That's a commandment, Mr. Nate. We've talked about this."

I turn to Samantha K, who's humming as she brushes her long auburn hair. "Finish up in the ladies' room, come on."

The Kims are a recent trend. As in Kardashian. The center used to be bursting with Elvises, Marilyn Monroes, and dead presidents, people with cultural gravitas. Now it's more of a superficial craziness. Choosing Kim K, if in fact anybody chooses their crazy, serves the same purpose as an inflatable sumo suit; though it looks completely ridiculous, it does absorb the bumps.

My boss, Tim, likes to say that our clients have a lot of psychology, which is like saying only storms count as weather. I prefer to think that we all have equal amounts of psychology, just maybe not the same kind. My kind includes a steady tendency to get too involved in things that don't concern me with intermittent delusions that a beautiful, much younger crazy woman might want me. Not to justify my attraction to Samantha K, but those feelings just come all on their own. I tell myself that I would never act on them.

I follow Samantha K into the hallway where our only Elvis is leaning against the opposite wall, thumbs hooked into the pockets of his jeans. "Darlin', don't you make that poor boy cry," Chinese Elvis says. He curls his lip and does his hair like Mr. Presley, but lucky for us he doesn't sing, and he never says, *you ain't nothin' but a hound dog*, the way Bearded Elvis used to.

Samantha K strides up to Chinese Elvis until her cinnamon cocoa eyes are looking down at him. "Maybe next time I'll make *you* cry, Chinese Elvis." I believe she has no intent either to frighten or turn him on, but Chinese Elvis's face shows both. She walks off toward the women's wing and I continue to the central atrium for the briefing in Tim's office.

To address the Kims' therapeutic needs, Tim moved the center from Anaheim into the mountains near Big Bear, away from the artifice of the city and the entertainment industry. It seemed like a good idea, but now the Salton Sea is nearly dry and a forest fire is approaching.

When I walk into his office, Tim and the two therapists, Roger and Amanda, are already seated at the small table in front of the corner picture windows.

"Nate, I know you had a lot of weather growing up in the Midwest, but I bet you've never seen anything like this," says Tim. He's staring at the trees after which the center is named. He calls *The Cedars* his baby, but it'll be his ass if it burns. "These winds continue their current intensity and direction, the fire could be in the adjacent canyon by morning," he says. "That'll be our cue to evac to the middle school."

I follow his gaze out the windows. The southern ridge is visible between the cedar tips, and flurries of ash brush against the windows as they swirl out of the gunmetal sky. Tim has a keen nose for the business of crazy. His market research deftly predicted the prolonged trend toward a low-culture crazy, but he ignored climate trends. I imagine fire cresting the ridge, cascading down the canyon walls like a tsunami. The hills burning out these big windows could be therapeutic for the Kims, but first they would have to notice.

"Second on the agenda is an update on the rationing. Nate?" Tim looks at me.

"Meters show a reduction in usage of nineteen percent, but the Kims are still sneaking water when they can," I say. "Not fans of letting it mellow—big surprise—and still exceeding their allotted shower time."

"Still taking extra showers with the messiahs?"

"Yep, though it's unclear whether that actually wastes water. Certainly has the incidental benefit of getting the messiahs to shower."

The counselors laugh. I think it's funny too except when it's Samantha K, but at least I don't blame her for my jealousy. Which is how I know I'm not crazy.

"This is no joke today," Tim says. "I'll keep all of you posted on the position of the fire. Nate, I want a briefing with the folks this afternoon – an update on the fire and review of the plan." He hands me the list of items to go into the evac bags.

On the way out, he catches me by the arm. "Samantha's family called today. Looks like her sister's death is imminent, if she wants to call."

"I'll speak with her."

Counselor Amanda says that disclosure of bad news is therapeutic for the Kims. Unlike the messiahs, who embrace tragedy as a sign of hope that the end is near, the Kims steadfastly refuse to acknowledge it.

Samantha K's sister Lauren, who has been battling breast cancer for years, came to say goodbye two weeks ago. Unaware that they were in the conference room, I walked in to set up for a staff lunch. They had turned their chairs toward each other, sitting knee to knee between the table and the far wall. Lauren was crying and Samantha K hugged her, an appropriately empathetic response, but when I set out the marbled cheese cubes and veggie trays from Costco, Samantha K said, "Hey, free samples." She strolled around the table with the delight of a country girl plucking wildflowers, leaving Lauren behind with her face in her hands.

I stand in the doorway of the community room. The messiahs don't normally congregate, as they tend to regard each other as charlatans, but they are now clustered in front of CNN in the TV corner. Wolf Blitzer is standing in front of a giant map of major wildfires in the West, each represented by an animated icon. Must be two dozen. As he explains that forest fires create their own weather, a holographic blaze ignites around him. Winds rush perimeter to center and a tree flies over Wolf's head, its roots weakened by years of drought. As pyrocumulus clouds form, a column of air shimmers behind Wolf, a vortex filled by an upswelling of whirling air. Just then, fire is drawn from either side of Wolf into the column, a firenado corkscrewing upward. The messiahs clap for joy.

Abraham Lincoln, our only president at the moment, is playing chess with Chinese Elvis, and the Kims, who would benefit the most from watching CNN, are instead sprawled on the couches in the conversation corner.

"Show it off," a Kim shouts.

Samantha K pops up and spins for the others, wearing a low reveal blouse tied off above her yoga pants. Late day sunlight streams through the window behind her, her figure nearly flattening to silhouette. Her auburn hair looks especially dark, except at the edges where her curls flare orange in the sunrays.

"Mmm, someone's been to DASH. Nice ass, girl," says Tanya K, who stands and wiggles her hips next to Samantha K. "No, yours is more Khloe," shouts another Kim from the couch.

Nobody wants to be a Khloe, so now a handful of Kims are actually snorting, they're laughing so hard. Like feral cats in a highway median, the credit that you give this particular group of Kims for living this long does nothing to mitigate the possibility that they'll perish at any moment.

Messiah Max sidles up to me. "I can see her camel toe, if you catch my drift." The messiahs are not ivory tower priests. Most have lived on the streets, exposing them to both the vilest and the most noble of human behavior, but as the Kims say, they can be whiny bitches. The yoga pants are a daily complaint.

"What do I always tell you?" I ask him.

He leans in to gaze at me over his glasses. "But how can I not look?"

"Ah, the allure of immodesty, am I right?"

Messiah Max cracks a smile as he stares again at Samantha K's camel toe. Now a few Kims are dancing and I hear Tanya K say, "TGIF girls." Samantha K sees me watching and sits down. She's self-conscious, I imagine, maybe even embarrassed, qualities that I never see in the other Kims.

Abraham Lincoln likes to call meetings to order, so I give him the sign. He's very formal. Wearing a black suit coat over black Dickies, he stands like a tall man though he couldn't be more than five-eight. He clears his throat. "Ladies and gentlemen, may I please have your attention. Mr. Nate has important things to say." He sits with a look of mission accomplished on his face, but the din continues unabated. He holds his breath and his cheeks paunch like a whoopee cushion that soon pops. "Tittie suckers!" he blurts.

Across the chessboard, Chinese Elvis laughs and says, "Fantastic." Counselor Roger suspects that Chinese Elvis is transitioning to Donald Trump.

As I update everyone on the progress of the fire, the feral Kims completely disregard me. They flash each other their nails and shoot the messiahs salacious looks. Chinese Elvis tries to get into it, but he's too eager for them.

"Everyone will need to pack a bag just in case we have to evacuate," I say. Samantha K volunteers to pass out the packing list. When she gets to Messiah Jack, her shower partner from just a few hours ago, his face reddens and he looks down. "The first stage of the evac will be to the middle school in town. If needed, we'll go back to the city." *If needed* means if the fire destroys the Cedars.

Messiah Gary stands and blurts, "We must always be prepared, for as the true book says, the Lord will come like a thief in the night." Messiah Jack and Messiah Max, not to be outdone, also stand and shout bible verses. I quickly dismiss everyone.

The conversation corner bursts into motion as the Kims stand. "TGIF in the North, girls!" calls out Tanya K.

Abraham Lincoln turns as though he's too bothered not to. "Not every day can be TGIF. That's the whole point—the F stands for Friday. Friday Friday fuck fuck."

Samantha K calmly strides up to Abraham Lincoln, who is hemmed in by the game table and the wall. Her face is gentle, loving even—not unlike the placid countenance of the Virgin Mary. She places a palm on his cheek, extends her long slender fingers under his ear, and he suddenly looks terrified. "Then thank God today, Abe, 'cause it's Friday."

It's Tuesday, but I stay out of it.

The nine Kims mesmerize me as they process toward the door. Each is yammering about something—who has the best selfie lips, what colors look best on North—each completely oblivious to all of the fires big and small that could immolate her at any moment. I find myself admiring their indomitable pursuit of what they want, even if it is absurdly contextualized as what they think Kim K would do. Samantha K looks at me sheepishly, another of her apparently lucid moments when she sees how inane the Kims are.

"Kim, may I speak with you?" I ask her.

She moves her long hair behind an ear with her right hand and lets the other Kims move past her into the hall.

"Your family called today. Lauren's not doing well." This might not even be sad for her, but then again maybe it's so painful that she can't deal with it. Full disclosure is best. "She's going to pass away soon. Do you understand?"

She stares at me for a few beats, expressionless in the way that people sometimes are just before erupting into sobs. "Thank you so much for telling me." She hugs me in an excessive showing of gratitude and walks into the hall.

I'm still staring at the now empty doorway, still feeling her body pressing into mine, still smelling her lavender shampoo, when I realize that Messiah Max is standing at my elbow. He's studying my face. Was I just looking at Samantha K's ass as she walked out? Might have been.

"Sinning begets sinning. It's a scourge that punishes all of us," he says. He leans in closer. "Even you."

WWKD? Have fun, rules be damned. WWJD? Kill everyone's buzz.

Truth to truth, Messiah Max sees my struggle. Science can explain the weather of a wildfire but nothing can account for why I'm attracted to a woman who thinks she's Kim Kardashian—a client, no less. I tell myself that it's only because Samantha K has a chance to get well. Before going to bed, I call her father to alert him of a possible evacuation and to ask him to call me directly with any news.

Around midnight, I wake to Tim looming over my bed. *This is it*, he says in a strained voice. Twenty minutes later, Abe Lincoln holds open the door as we step outside into a ring of floodlight, wind crashing like the ocean through the treetops. Smoke and flakes of ash sweep across the clearing before disappearing into pitch-black imagination beyond the arc of light.

As they board the bus, the Kims grimace like teenagers off to school, but the messiahs are gleeful. Messiah Jack stands in the aisle and addresses everyone with the authority of a schoolteacher giving instructions on a field trip. "Peter 3 Verse 10: The heavens will disappear with a roar; the elements will be destroyed by fire, and the Earth and everything in it will be laid bare." He had a *told you so* tone. It's a wonder we still have so many messiahs; despite all the horrible things happening in the world, the end never comes. Must be disillusioning.

Tim takes roll on his clipboard as I steer us down the gravel drive. From there, it's slow going on a narrow road that climbs through the curves. Abe Lincoln is seated behind me. He asks to make an announcement, then rises to his knees to face the back of the bus—something about perseverance and fortitude of heart. All that's visible of the Kims are a few feet sticking into the aisle at the back of the bus. Tim is also nodding off, even the Messiahs, as exciting as the promise of the end must be for them.

The road levels on the ridge where it snakes for several minutes. We come to a curve where there's a view of the succession of canyons to the south. I pull off and marvel at the wide swath of orange that burns in the distance. I think I'm the only one awake, so I linger. The forest shimmers gorgeously like the breathing embers of a campfire. It draws me in until I lose perspective of distance and danger. A solitary voice emerges from the darkness behind me. *And I saw what looked like a sea of glass glowing with fire.* Suddenly, an orange plume rises from the middle of that sea, a column of fire that whirls upward. Flames flicker skyward like electric tongues, and it dawns on me—a firenado. Jump-started by fear, I gas the engine and soon we're descending into the next canyon toward our refuge.

The school custodian shakes his head as we file off the bus, and I'm not sure if he's shaking it at the fire, at having to report to work at this hour, or at all the psychology. We follow him to a door that leads directly to the gym.

The gym is stuffy and reeks of varnish, but with the bleachers pushed in there's plenty of floor space. Tim immediately commandeers the PE teacher's office and the Kims take over the corner farthest from anything useful like the locker room and drinking fountain. I locate the gym mats and emergency blankets, and though it takes a while for everyone to settle, especially the messiahs, eventually all falls quiet.

I have first watch. I slide a stack of mats to the light outside the locker rooms and plop down with a crossword, my back against the cinderblock wall. I set my phone next to me and think about the fire rising into the sky. Drought is weather, and the firenado or whatever that was, that's weather too. My phone buzzes—Samantha K's father. "Lauren passed away tonight," he says. I tell him I'm sorry for his loss. We talk about the evacuation and I promise to break the sad news to Samantha. "Let's hope it is," he says.

Time passes slowly. Tim comes out of the office at 2:00 to relieve me but I shake him off and he disappears again behind the office door. Somewhere near 5:00, a figure rises in the Kim corner, a silhouette that plods the length of the basketball court toward me. The first light of day enters dimly through the windows above the wall of bleachers. Even before I can see her face, her long unhurried stride tells me that it's Samantha K. I expect her to walk on to the bathroom, but she sits next to me on the mats. There's no reason for her to be up except that she's being pulled into the firestorm, uprooted like a tree to feel the pain of the flames.

Her eyes peer at me between ribbons of hair that have fallen across her face.

"Your father called," I say. "Lauren passed last night."

She nods as though this isn't news, then averts my gaze. "She wasn't in any pain." Not sure why I say it, a lie to comfort someone who needs no comforting, but then she leans into me and her arms are suddenly wrapped around me. I struggle to stay upright, trying to assess what's happening as her chest heaves against mine and her breath warms my neck. She squeezes tight and I squeeze right back.

She pulls away, big watery eyes, hands on my chest. "I haven't been a good sister," she says. Sobs come. She buries her face in my shoulder to staunch the flow. It feels good to be important to her even if just for a moment, as though she really sees me. When she lifts her head again, she looks past me to the girls' locker room.

"Shower?" I ask.

She nods, then stares at me as though waiting to see if I'm coming. Not as though she wants me to, but as though that might be the only way she'll get a shower, and that's just the most depressing thing.

"Go ahead," I tell her. "Long as you want."

Soon after she goes in, I hear the water and I marvel at her sadness. At least I think she was sad.

A voice comes from on high. "Now is the time thou has waited for. Ready yourselves, for today we return to the lake of fire." While I was distracted by Samantha K, Messiah Robert apparently clambered to the mountaintop that is the retracted bleachers. He now stands in the fog of gray light that comes through the windows.

Just then, the office door bursts open. Tim flicks on the gym lights and walks to center court. "Everybody circle up!" He claps his rally hands like a PE coach. It takes a few minutes for Messiah Robert to climb down and the others to gather. "Good news—the evac order's been lifted. Seems the winds have reversed direction." He looks at the messiahs to say, "It's a real-life miracle, I tell you what."

Tim has the joy of a new believer, but the messiahs aren't pleased. The expression on their faces reminds me of how I felt as a kid after a busted snowstorm, when I expected a snow day but woke to grass and wet pavement.

"Pack it up—let's get some breakfast," Tim says. More rally hands.

I step outside. Across the parking lot, bands of brilliant reds and oranges radiate from the tree line ahead of the coming sun. I bring the bus around, anxious to be back in the gym when Samantha K comes out of the locker room.

When I return, Chinese Elvis and the messiahs are lined up at the gym door behind Tim and Abe Lincoln. They walk out to the bus, but the cluster of Kims is lagging behind. At the yawn of the locker room door, I turn my back on their approaching chatter—something about waist training and revenge bodies—to see Samantha K emerge with bare feet and wet hair.

She walks straight for me, until her toes nearly touch my boots. "How are you doing?" I ask. Her swollen eyes meet mine and her lips part as though about to speak. After her lucidity a short time ago, I'm eager to hear what she might now say, but the other Kims are nearly upon us.

"Champagne breakfast in my room, girl!" Tanya K yells behind me.

Samantha K's gaze strays from my face to somewhere over my shoulder and she slips past me. I turn and squint to see her merge with the other Kims, the rising sun now obliterating the doorframe. Sunbeams erase Samantha K's wet footprints step by step from the gym floor behind her. As she steps outside, light catches like wildfire in the cinnamon edges of her hair, then engulfs her completely.

poem

Breakfast Devotional

lawrence di stefano

Because there is no definite answer
that I can conjure,
I look for one
in the golden
yolks of this morning's eggs,
all of which have broken
in the black pan—
all three bleeding into the clear,
now whitening glair
that suspended them.
Today won't be any easier,
I read in the mess
of egg, the white shells in the claw
of my other hand.
I want to put them back together
and begin again,
but now it's all compounding.
Can you hear me?
The kitchen air thickens
with a scream
My neighbor across the canyon
keeps exotic birds
in what I imagine
are cages too small.

I've learned the parrot does not
sing as the birds sing,
   but screams like a human,
pressing their hand upon the hot
wrought iron—no
            discernible answer,
            though I remain
            as silent as you,
   a question mark
         hunched over this
               little blue flame.

I don't know if I could
            believe in anything that does
            not feel the same
                        kind of pain.

The Willows:
California Cool in Calorific California

eric bryan

Sun-punished Interstate 5 reached out straight north and shimmered in the hot distance. I pulled off past a willow tree into an old one-story town, twenty-five miles southwest of Chico: Willows, California; one hundred and twelve degrees Fahrenheit. I was here for the U.S. Forest Service's "Basic 32"—thirty-two hours of wild-land firefighter training. The ill-conceived plan was that I would be one of the only freelance writers on the frontlines of wildfires throughout the Western States, enabling me to sell my dispatches to newspapers and magazines for staggering sums.

I drove over the cracked, oozing asphalt to the motel, my oasis. My room was at the far end of the complex on the ground floor. I pressed the key into the lock, stepped into the cool dimness, and dropped my bag. I fell crosswise on the bed and was lulled by the breathing background drone of the air-conditioning. Air-conditioning hummed throughout Willows; it was a matter of survival.

The textured ceiling sparkled in the shadows with flecks of gold glitter. It reminded me of childhood travels throughout California, and motel rooms like this one. On those trips, we drove past mile after mile of corn and sunflowers, and the land stretched out far and wide—golden, open, and beautiful.

In the Old West, a mile east of present Willows was the only landmark between settlements on the Sacramento River and the western foothills: a spring-fed watering hole bordered with willow trees. Hill-bound travelers from Princeton used to navigate by "the Willows." This spot, on Willow Creek, was the only live watering place between Cache Creek in Yolo County to the south and Stony Creek on the north. Enterprising pioneer-settler Granville P. Swift took it over in the late 1840s and charged area cattlemen for use of the oasis.

"The best photo I ever got was when a VW bus drove straight into a restaurant across the street from my apartment. I took the pictures without even leaving the room!" So said Eddie, a part-time photojournalist I met during training. We were sitting beside the motel pool. He worked for Pacific Gas & Electric in San Francisco and was trying to break into full-time freelance photography. He thought that frontline fire pictures would invigorate his career.

"I drive this little truck around on calls for PG&E," Eddie went on, "and I keep my camera on the seat next to me, loaded, primed, and ready to go. I watch for fires, UFOs, you name it. I snap away, and then sell the pictures to newspapers."

"And PG&E has no idea?"

"Are you kidding?" Eddie leaned his long lanky frame toward me in the blinding sun and jabbed the air between us with his index finger. "Sometimes you've got to dog it to get anywhere, you've *got* to. Do you think these corporations care about us? They'll take us any way, any day, and *every* day they can. And they *do*. I'm not going to slave for life for someone else." His clean-shaven face relaxed slightly. "Look, this job is a tool I use to pay the rent and a platform to boost my photography. Otherwise, I'm nowhere. Nowhere!"

Eddie and I drove to an old-fashioned Willows supermarket and bought some round, seedless watermelons. We brought them back to the pool area, sat down with the melons cool in our laps, and looked at each other: We realized we had no way of slicing the gourds.

Eddie picked his melon up and carried it over to a large, decorative volcanic rock and carefully bashed it against the rock until it split open. Performing this maneuver wearing only his swimming trunks, and with his brass-colored hair hanging down his back in a long ponytail, created an archaic-looking spectacle. He cradled one jagged melon half to himself in a caveman crouch, squinted over his shoulder suspiciously at me, uttered a prehistoric grunt and buried his face in the fruit. When he finished the first half, he paused, leered at me primitively, his face shining with watermelon juice, and grabbed the other half of the melon. I could scarcely eat from choking with laughter.

In Basic 32 class we learned of some of the lesser-known hazards of wildfires: Fire-heated rocks loosened by the blaze which roll downhill and ignite new fires; charging animals, including rattlesnakes, fleeing the flames; and "widow-makers," large limbs or parts of trees which fall on firefighters before, during, or after fires. The most sinister danger of all, we were told, was being uphill from a fire, a predicament which spells almost certain death: you can't outrun a wildfire raging its way uphill. We chanted the wild-land firefighter's safety mantra:

"Look up; look down; look around."

We watched films, we read handouts, and we listened to lectures. Amongst our materials was a workbook called "Standards for Survival." On the cover was a reassuring illustration of a flaming skull wearing a firefighter's helmet. But most alarming to me, as I flipped through the booklet, was the omission of pages 21 and 22, and 31 and 32. Was potentially life-saving information missing? One of our instructors, a large, bespectacled, mustachioed jokester, informed us of the rivalry between government agencies. Elaborating slightly on this point, he told us that California Department of Forestry employees refer to the United States Forest Service as the United States Forest Circus. "But don't worry," he said through a chuckle, "we call the CDF Coffee and Doughnuts Forever."

Eddie and I walked to a sandwich shop for lunch. The heat, now at one hundred-and-thirteen degrees, was such that I couldn't believe the tires of the parked cars weren't melting against the asphalt they rested upon. Every building I entered in Willows was powerfully air-conditioned and stepping inside one of them from the solar-blasted streets and sidewalks was like treading over a heated stovetop into a refrigerator.

"A writer?" Eddie asked after we'd finished our sandwiches and lemonade and were strolling back to the classroom. "Look, I knew a couple of writers. One built himself a tiny writing nook under a staircase. He wrote articles full-time, and the way he survived was by selling each one twenty to fifty times to papers all over the country. And then there was the novelist. He lived on the beach. He'd get up early, run on the sand, swim, then go in for breakfast. After that he'd write till mid-afternoon, then relax with a few drinks. That was his daily regimen, and he did all right."

Back in my room late that afternoon I read up a little on pioneer-settler Granville P. Swift and Willows-area history. Swift came west over the plains in 1843 and arrived in California via Oregon with the Kelsey party. He took part in Sutter's campaign in 1845, was involved in the Bear Flag Revolt, and served as captain in 1846 in Fremont's California Battalion.

Swift built an adobe home about seventeen miles north of Willows and became a cattle baron. He amassed great droves of cattle and hired Indian vaqueros for the annual herding. He held rodeos at his adobe and at the Murdock Ranch west of Willows and is known for planting the first North Sacramento Valley barley.

When gold was found at Bidwell Bar on the Feather River southeast of Chico, Swift reportedly made a fortune by hiring large crews of Stony Creek Indians to pan the river. Legend tells that he buried his fortune in gold dust around his adobe, a tale that has attracted treasure hunters for over a century. In 1854, Swift moved to Sonoma County, but his name lives on in Willows' Glenn County: Swift's Point, a once fordable place on the Sacramento River, is near Hamilton City, several miles east of Orland.

In the 1870s, when the Central Pacific Railroad extended its lines north to Oregon, the town of Willows was born. It became the shipping depot for surrounding wheat and barley ranches and was named county seat in 1891.

"Now listen," Eddie said, leaning forward across the dinner table and pointing his fork at me, "what I'm after is freedom. And to be free in this world you first need financial freedom." This was the eve of our day of field training, and we'd decided to have dinner at the motel restaurant. The place was oddly grand for a small-town motel eatery: High-ceilinged, with lots of exposed wood—timbers and railings—and even an indoor stream which bubbled over crushed quartzite and ran under an arched wooden footbridge.

"I've been thinking about this," Eddie whispered. "Here's one way to do it: Get a cabin out on a remote part of the coast. Cultivate two pot plants in amongst the redwoods. Every day make sure they've got enough water and light. Then, after several months, once they're fully mature and are covered with buds, sell them for fifty-thousand dollars cash each."

This was in the days before the wave of legalization initiatives and legislation, so for plants perhaps ten feet tall and ten pounds in weight, Eddie's black-market valuations were feasible. But mentally going down the list of things which might go wrong, I could only think of how his scheme was riddled with risk. I kept on chewing.

"What? Are you philosophically opposed to marijuana?" Eddie asked.

"I'm philosophically opposed to going to jail. And besides, what kind of underworld character is going to give you $100,000 cash? Don't you think he'd rather knock you over the head or shoot you and get your plants for free?"

Eddie laughed, and the waitress walked over to our table. I asked her what flavor of Jell-O she had.

"Red," she replied, as though she were telepathically aware of my color-flavor synesthesia.

"Oh yeah," piped in Eddie, "I like to order my food by color." He put his hand thoughtfully to his chin. "Now let me see, I'll have a white milk, a black steak, and a red Jell-O."

For our field training we were issued the following pieces of equipment: helmet; goggles; gloves; miner's headlamp; four extra batteries; Meal-Ready-to-Eat; file; fire resistant shirt; fire resistant trousers; four one-quart bottles; first-aid kit; and most menacingly, one fire shelter. Looking like something developed by NASA for outer-space campouts, this last item was a sort of foil blanket which firefighters cover themselves with should they be trapped by flames. All this gear was carried in a big red rectangular backpack.

The field training was conducted at Alder Springs in the Mendocino National Forest in the Coast Range. Eddie and I drove west out of Willows along California State Highway 162. The flatlands of Willows soon gave way to undulating hills covered with dry grass and dotted with grand live oak trees—classic California savannah. Dusty cattle wandered along and over the hills, and we passed the occasional solitary, steel-tower windmill, the kind that is found creaking forlornly on remote American ranchlands.

"Do you know what most people spend their lives doing?" Eddie hadn't spoken since we'd left Willows, but he'd been staring disgustedly back and forth between the road and the landscape, and I knew something was brewing. He stuck his elbow out the window and went on. "I'm going to tell you. Most people spend their lives saying things they don't mean and doing things they don't want to do. I won't have it. Do you realize—look, this is ridiculous. I'm almost forty. I need the freedom of open space, of travel, of living the way I want to live. I have got to break out. *Break out!*"

Twenty miles west of Willows we crossed Stony Creek, the only water we'd seen to quench this vast dryness. Our thirst magnified by the heat, the clear water looked cold and fresh as it spilled over turquoise rocks and sipped its way through the parched hill-fields.

We turned off onto a gravel Forest Service road and made our way into the mountains. The air cooled as we climbed, and by the time we reached Alder Springs in amongst the pine trees, it was comfortable. We changed into our fire clothes, were given a choice of shovel, rake, or Pulaski (a hoe/ pick and axe combination tool named for the firefighter who invented it) and were led into the pine forest to make a fire line. Our instructor was a gnarled smoke jumper, who with his stout physique, scruffy beard and red, swollen nose, looked like some variety of forest-dwelling gnome.

There were fifteen trainees in our group. We dug our fire line (maybe best described as a fire break, a rough six to eight-foot wide swath made by clearing the ground of flammables and run out long enough to stop or contain a fire) along the hilly forest floor, covering thousands of feet in short order.

Eddie, of course, was a one-man firefighting machine. He dug, he chopped, and he raked like a champion, as though believing in his very soul that the flames were raging ever nearer. He hacked furiously at "smol-dering" roots and shoveled dirt at "sparking" tree trunks until his ill-fitting helmet slipped forward over his face and he fell over backwards with an almighty clatter of tools and equipment.

Our final lesson was devoted to the proper implementation of the dreaded fire shelter. This is a last resort device, used only when there is no escape route. To deploy the fire shelter, pull it from the pack, unroll it, hold it over and behind the body, step into the lower end, and pulling the shelter along with you, fall to the ground. The shelter must be in contact with the earth all the way around you. The concept is that when the approaching wall of flame encounters the nonflammable shelter and finds no fuel to burn, it passes or leaps over it—with you concealed beneath—and continues on its way.

Fire shelters have saved lives, but they sometimes fail in unusually high-heat situations. "If you need your fire shelter," the smoke jumper gnome warned, "it's probably too late for you." Never need it; that was the key.

"Remember, to be free, you need financial freedom," Eddie told me as we stood in the parking lot the next morning. "If you come up with any big money ideas less risky than mine, give me a call." He got into his van, squealed out onto the road, and turned south. The early sun glinted off his tinted windows as he thrust one arm out, waved, and disappeared into the breaking California day. Thinking of his PG&E-supported photography and his quick-income scheme, I wondered what would ever become of Eddie.

Standing there reflecting on the completed thirty-two hours of training, I reached into my shirt pocket and pulled out my officially issued Incident Qualification Card, more commonly known as a Fire Card. The card was red, and under Qualifications, "Firefighter" had been typed. In the box marked Additional Skills it read, "National Geographic Film Crew."

I got in my car and drove away feeling a mixture of melancholy and release over being a lone traveler once again. The sun was sliding the shadows out from between the hills and the dusty cattle were on the march through the rolling savannah.

It wasn't long before the Sacramento Valley heated up. I was driving on a deserted side road, getting thirsty, but all I could see around me were the baked ranchlands. My new firefighting equipment was in the back, and something had been rolling around on the floor behind me. An oak spread halfway across the road ahead, so I decided to pull over in the shade, cool off, and investigate the noise.

I got out, opened the back door, and looked inside, puzzled. I'd thought we'd only bought two of these, one for each of us. I shrugged and smiled to myself. Feeling earthy, basic, almost primitive, I reached in and gently picked up the plump, cool gourd off the floor of the car, and carrying it greedily, lovingly, looked around for the nearest large rock.

Road Trip Nouveau

laton carter

In 1983 a band named Kajagoogoo was popular. It was summer, and the boy was still too young for a driver's permit. This meant he would sit in the back seat listening to his one cassette on the Walkman he had inherited from his older brother as his parents navigated across the country to their home state of South Dakota. For them, the trip would be filled with mixed emotions and faces from the past. For the boy, scenes from the prairie—unfamiliar relatives, milky tap water, Russian olive trees, root cellars—would be understood through the prism of Kajagoogoo. He had inherited the cassette as well.

Uncle Len was not his uncle but great uncle. He hadn't smoked a pipe like the boy's grandfather had, and as a result was still alive. Len was somewhere around eighty and still rode a tractor. The boy had only seen tractors from a distance while traversing the interstate corridor with his mother on school days. The work appeared full of dust, and the boy wondered if tractor operators listened to anything in their glass-encased cabs. *You're old enough, aren't you, young man?* Uncle Len dangled a pair of keys from his fingers. This was the boy's introduction to heavy machinery. It would be the first combustion engine vehicle he had driven.

Leighton Buzzard is a town in Bedfordshire, England. A waiter named Christopher opened his waitstaff book and wrote down his last name— *Hamill*—and then looked at it. There were two L's. He spelled the name backward, moved one of the L's to the end, and came up with *Limahl*, which made Christopher smile. This would be the name he'd become famous by. Like Cher, *Limahl* would be mononymic. It was just a matter of finding a band to back him.

After dinner, Uncle Len let his wife do the dishes. It was time to shower. Upon reappearing in the front room, Len was clad in an untied bathrobe and red silk briefs. His chest was covered in gray hair. *Leonard!* said his wife and hurried back to the kitchen. Uncle Len chuckled and positioned himself for falling backward into an easy chair. The Naugahyde made an *oomph* sound when he did. *These make me feel sexy*, Len stated plainly, and nodded.

The band was called *Art Nouveau*, and its members appeared to wear Pomeranians—electrocuted and fluffy and teased with product—on their heads. Limahl wore a Pomeranian too, he'd be perfect center stage, but the band's name wasn't right. It should be something that stood out, something with avant-garde currency, and so Limahl proposed the generic sounds of a baby: *Gaga-goo-goo*. Still, it needed a twist. Limahl got out his waitstaff book and carefully wrote down each phoneme in equally-spaced capital letters: GA GA GOO GOO. He crossed out the first two consonants and began entering substitutes. MA MA GOO GOO sounded incestuous. KA KA GOO GOO was funny at first, but ultimately juvenile. Limahl stared at the letters, tapping the eraser end of the pencil against his lips. Kaka-googoo? Almost. He crossed out the second K, substituted a J in its place, and a band was born: Kajagoogoo it would be.

Lillian was Uncle Len's college-aged granddaughter, and the spare room on the top floor was reserved for her when she visited on weekends or during breaks at SDSU. There was a dresser, full-length mirror, reading lamp, and twin bed. A circular hook-braided rug took up the remaining floor space. This is where the boy would sleep. It felt oddly erotic to be in a girl's room. The boy knew he was related to this person—a second cousin or cousin once removed—but he had never met Lillian, had never even heard his parents mention her name, and so the boy felt she could be any girl. What did she look like? There wasn't a photograph around to tell. The boy sat down on the bed. He imagined a girl with a Pomeranian on her head and wearing a Ralph Lauren sweater, 501s, and penny loafers. What bands did she like?

The top drawer of the dresser was empty. The second drawer had a throw blanket and bible. The third had thermal underwear and sweaters that appeared hand-knit. The fourth drawer—the boy hadn't known what he was looking for, but this was it. In the back, behind a flannel robe and neatly folded into a square: a single pair of cotton panties. The boy pulled them out. They were white with pink polka dots, size medium. Lillian wore panties. What should he do? The boy held the panties up to the reading lamp. Opaque. He looked into the mirror. He was holding panties. Unbuttoning his jeans, he regarded his own underwear. They were plain in comparison: a thick elastic band with two pointless stripes, brown and blue, running the length of the waist, and a fly that never got used. Had Lillian ever worn these fourth drawer panties? They seemed new. Slowly the boy stepped out of his own, a cold electricity charging his follicles. He held his breath and put a foot through, then the other.

Two Houses

katherine van eddy

Late summer, my kids and I
sit on the porch swing
watching the trucks demolish
the home across the street.
Asbestos in the walls, mistakes
of the past, means the whole
structure has to come down.
At first, it's thrilling, so unnatural.
Machinery strong enough
to break bricks, metal claws
rip apart the roof.

A mile away, ten years earlier,
I'm crying in the kitchen
of a two-bedroom apartment,
wiping the counters, the dishes
drying in the rack, leftovers
portioned in the fridge.
He's watching television
and I'm wondering,
Is this all there is?

After the roof, the walls are easy.
It takes days to pull it apart
and months to rebuild.
The workers continue
even through snow and ice.
We'll move before we see it finished.

We filled our first home with things
I didn't want to look at:
the kitchen table and chairs
he bought used with stains and wear.
The shower curtain I had to return twice
before I found one without a strange smell.
Through the French doors to the deck,
our fifty dollar grill already rusted
after only one use.
Beneath the awning,
still too much exposure
to the rain.

My mother and the mother of my husband Larry Behrendt move to Paris in 1958 according to an alternative timeline

stephanie barbé hammer

You heard me, Larry.

Instead of sitting in a Long Island rambler (your mother) or a Manhattan apartment (my mother) with depression and cancer (both our mothers) and husbands who never come home for dinner because they work for their fathers (your father) or who drink and see another woman (my father), our mothers, Charlotte Behrendt and Barbé Hammer, pack up their bags and move to Paris, France.

Larry, you have maintained in a previous conversation that there are obstacles to making this alternative history work as a believable narrative.

Barbé knows but hates speaking French, you observe. Charlotte probably knows a little French but also probably hates speaking it. They both hate looking stupid. They both have problematic relationships with other women. With most people.

"But Larry," I say, "they need a change. They need to meet in 1958 when I am four and you are three3."

"How?" you want to know.

"Hey! They both like art, so….maybe they meet at MOMA?"

"But they are both so shy," you say.

"Yes, we'll need some sort of inciting incident. What if Charlotte drops her purse or one of her gloves? Or maybe Barbé can't find the ladies' room—"

"Wait—" you say. "She never uses a public restroom. Never."

"Ok—let me think…."

What about if Charlotte tries to get a taxi outside the museum? She is standing there waving at the darting yellow cars, and Barbé comes out of the museum and sees her. *This woman is so beautiful*, Barbé thinks, *and she wears her hair up*, which she, Barbé, can never manage. She also admires that Charlotte is wearing a store-bought dress. Barbé's father designs her clothes, and she's sick of not being able to choose the fabric or the color or the cut. Besides, Charlotte looks like Mary Tyler Moore. Endearing!

"Excuse me," Barbé says to Charlotte, in a surprisingly low voice, because she's taken acting, and thought about acting as a career, but the actual auditions are frightening and the entire process, except for being on stage itself, is too terrifying to consider.

Charlotte turns fearfully because being an American woman in the 50s, even if you're white, requires a certain continual fear. Moreover, she's much smarter than everyone she knows, including her father who didn't want her to go to college, but she got a full scholarship to the University of Chicago so what *could* he do? Still, she dreads that moment when people realize how smart she is and think she's weird or stuck up or both.

But now she sees another pair of brown eyes like hers. Dark lustrous hair, like hers. A woman who is about the same height, although she is older. Which means more sophisticated, worldly. Entrancing!

"You can probably take the bus," Barbé tells Charlotte.

"The bus?" Charlotte says. She thought that if you were high class—which this woman obviously is, with her engagement ring made of artfully shaped sapphires and her clearly couture dress—you only took taxis.

"Sure," says Barbé. And because Charlotte looks like her and seems as lost as she often feels, she hazards another question. "Where are you going exactly?"

"Penn Station," is the answer.

Now Barbé lifts her chin with happiness, because one thing she knows like the back of her hand is the Manhattan transit system.

"This way," says Barbé. The women walk to 7th Avenue.

They rave about Chagall's *I and the Village* painting.

"Isn't there something jolly," says Barbé stepping carefully in her black patent high heels. "about that giant green face and that cow?"

"Chagall lived in Paris," Charlotte says. "I'd love to go there."

"The Parisians can be mean," Barbé says knowingly. She's been there as a kid with her dress designer parents.

Charlotte nods.

"So many people in the world are mean," she offers.

Barbé smiles as the bus lumbers down the crowded avenue.

"Thank you for your help," Charlotte says. "Perhaps…I'll see you at MOMA again?"

"I come during my lunch hour," says Barbé. "I'm secretary to a publisher."

"Office work is thrilling," says Charlotte.

They meet often and perambulate the still unexpanded, intimate museum.

"I don't like Picasso," Barbé confides. "The rose and blue periods are ok. But those later paintings. Let's face it: ugly."

Charlotte agrees. "I like Miró and Modigliani." Then she notes, "Funny, there aren't many women painters."

"Those fellas have all those creative mistresses, and the women don't have time to paint, because they are too busy being sexy all the time for the men," Barbé says.

"I want to live someplace where I don't have to be sexy for anybody," Charlotte says.

"Me too," says Barbé.

That does it. They decide on the spot to move to the sexiest city in the world. A city whose very streets ooze the hormones of a thousand years. You, as an individual, don't have to be sexy in a place like that. A place like that does all the work for you.

Our moms deplane at Paris-Orly (Charles de Gaulle airport hasn't been built yet) and they rent an apartment. Barbé reads books at the *Bibliothèque Nationale* because library reading is a good way to acclimate. Charlotte learns French in two months. She tries working in the American Embassy office, but Simone de Beauvoir comes in and insists that she get a Ph.D. in Poli Sci at the Sorbonne.

"*Elle est géniale,*" Simone exclaims to Jean Paul Sartre. Which means, "She's a genius."

"I'm happy just reading," Barbé says, but at the *chocolaterie* near the BN, she runs into the famous actor/director Jean Louis Barrault who also has a chocolate habit.

"*Parfaite!*" he exclaims, after he hears her order. "You don't need an audition. Just come and perform in *Rhinoceros* and other strange plays by Beckett and Sartre."

Barbé joins the company, remains withdrawn, but it's fine because everybody else in the theater is at least as weird as she is. She specializes in parts where she says nothing or everything. Albert Camus comes to produce a play before he dies in his automobile accident.

"I too am an outsider," he tells Barbé backstage, kissing her hand.

"I really liked how repellent Meursault is in *L'étranger*," she informs him shyly. He flashes his brilliant famous author smile. Someone finally understands his book.

Will our fathers come to Paris? Will your younger siblings be born? *Peut-être.*

But certainly, I'll move to Paris and live with my mother, and you, Larry—genius child—your mom will *send* for you.

We'll share one enormous apartment. We'll play in the *Jardin Luxembourg*, wearing matching sailor suits, which won't look stupid because we're suddenly European.

Envision us, Larry: childhood sweethearts with mothers who stroll the boulevards in their brilliance and black dresses, debating existentialism and theater of the absurd, celebrating Chagall, trashing Picasso, and gazing at the Paris Métro map boasting three hundred stations.

That last piece of information seduces you at last, and you concur with this new timeline, murmuring the following into my ear:

"This remarkable system enables one to commute rapidly between a host of locations, be it the #2 to *Sacré Coeur* or the #3 to *Père Lachaise Cemetery*, where Oscar Wilde is buried, but Jim Morrison—not yet.

Happy Birthday Deb

shira musicant

The cookies called to her: sweet little invitations. They sat on the plate and whispered her name. They cried out when she went into the next room. They shouted, they cajoled. They were butter and sugar ultimatums. After one, Deb had another. And another. After six cookies she knew she needed help. The force was not with her. She was powerless.

The doorbell rang and Julie walked in, a wine bottle protruding from her purse. A Cabernet. Julie wore a red scarf that looked familiar.

"Help," Julie said, "I need a corkscrew." She looked at Deb's face, dusted with sugar. "And I need cookies."

Julie glowed. She'd dyed her hair red and it now matched the scarf, which looked like Deb's scarf. *That's mine*, Deb thought. *Did I lend it to her?* Deb tried to think about something else. She tried to send her mind to a calm place.

She found the corkscrew and opened the wine. The wine began humming.

Julie ate most of the cookies. There were four left. She threw those in the trash.

"I'm saving you, Deb," she said. "They say that cookies are the new cigarettes."

Deb heard the cookies crying softly, under the humming. Then the humming got louder and Julie and Deb sat down on the living room floor. Their wine glasses promised berries, tobacco, and deep conversation. They clinked glasses. Deb took a deep, calming breath. If anyone could help her with Jack, it would be Julie.

"I'm losing him to a sailboat," Deb said. This situation was not addressed in the self-help book she'd been reading. She read a chapter on attitude and one on assertiveness and another on sending her mind to calm places. There was nothing in her self-help book on husbands who quit jobs and bought sailboats. "He wants to sail away, Julie. It's every man's dream, he says."

"It's the position of the stars and planets, Deb, the way they are lining up." Julie sipped her wine. "Mercury is in retrograde and that is often associated with transportation problems."

Deb supposed Jack's new sailboat *might* be considered a transportation problem. Julie was a Gemini. "But Jack doesn't even know how to swim." Deb thought that could be the transportation problem. "Maybe I should buy him swim lessons?"

The cat came into the living room, half of a lizard in his mouth, most of the upper half. He put it on the rug between them. Julie seemed indifferent. Deb considered taking the lizard to the trash but stroked the cat instead. She thought the cat might be an Aries, bold and fearless.

Jack, of course, was a Sagittarius.

"A fire sign," Julie said, "not one to consider how his actions will affect you. You need a calm mind."

The wine bottle hummed louder, a riveting little tune, promising carefree afternoons. Deb poured more into their glasses.

The cat rolled onto his side and stretched.

Julie gazed into her wine glass, as if reading Deb's future. "Wait till Mercury goes direct. Then listen to that little voice inside, and it will tell you what to do."

Deb hadn't always heard "that little voice inside," as Julie called it. However, she'd intended, as one of her self-improvement projects, to buy a book on cultivating intuition. Also, maybe a book on weight loss.

The cat hummed. The wine purred.

Julie brought a small box out of her purse. She opened it and pulled out a cupcake piled with chocolate frosting. She dug through her purse again and found a pink spiral birthday candle, which she stuck on top.

"For your birthday, Deb," she said. She lit the candle and lurched through the Happy Birthday song while Deb tried to form a birthday wish.

Deb blew out the birthday candle. Birthday wishes—unformed—hovered in the air above her. After the singing, they shared the cupcake. The frosting emitted a low moan, not the exercising or pain kind—the other kind.

Jack wandered into the living room and headed to the kitchen. He was wearing his new rubber-ducky boxer shorts, which Deb knew because that was all he was wearing. Julie appeared calm. Deb felt slightly agitated, not sure of the protocol when one's husband walked around in boxers in front of one's best friend. She mentally reviewed the chapters in her self-help book, and remembered nothing that would cover this situation. Jack came out of the kitchen with a wine glass. Julie poured. They were both calm. Jack looked at the lizard, and smiled at Julie.

"Nice scarf," he said, and touched its fringe.

"Thanks." Julie glowed brighter and smiled back at Jack.

Deb's wine glass called her. She swished and sipped, and looked inside for her calm place.

Jack looked at Deb. "Oh, yeah." He raised his glass. "Happy Birthday, Deb."

She had not found her calm place. Something moved inside her. She thought it might be a feeling—one of those her former therapist used to ask about. It started in her belly, red, like her scarf. It pulsed a drumbeat up and down her arms and legs.

She picked up the lizard with a napkin and took it to the kitchen. It did not protest. She dropped it into the trash. She took the cookies out of the trash. They whimpered as she brushed off some of the debris that had accumulated on the powdered sugar during their internment with her garbage. She put them on a plate. Small flecks of something now decorated the cookies.

Julie and Jack were sipping wine when she returned to the living room. They were quiet. Deb set the plate of cookies in front of Jack. He took one. Deb picked up her wine glass and looked inside. The wine and the remaining cookies were quiet, no humming, moaning, singing, or crying.

Deb listened to the quiet.

A little voice inside spoke. *Sail away, Jack. No swim lessons for you.*

The cat purred.

His One Small Comfort

tanner abernathy

I burn cigarettes in a bowl for my father.
I fill my kitchen with the hard smell
that would cling to his shirts and his chin
like lichen to stones.
I like to burn several at once.
I fan a hanky over the bowl and
stuff it in my back pocket,
wadding the hanky tightly like a white ball of cancer
before I leave the house,
carrying my father with me as I go about my day.

Oasis for Everything

ashley warren

I make beef stew for her and Boyfriend of twenty-three years. It's under-seasoned. I've never liked cooking.

They don't leave after dinner. They sit on the sofa watching "The Voice." Boyfriend digesting his second helping, and my mother falling asleep with her mouth open.

I keep looking over at her. She's sitting up with her head cocked back and her hands in her lap. She looks so dead—as if someone has picked up her lifeless body and propped it up on the couch.

This is why I'm here.

Her Parkinson's is getting worse and California isn't getting any better. So I came back. For now.

Her fragility is alarming. Her mouth is a cave and her body a crippled bird.

I look at her the way a child might who is observing a burn victim for the first time.

I'm overdue. Each day I clean and sort. I organize drawers, or bleach the counters, or wash her never worn clothes.

I make mobiles out of feathers and shells and cotton. I make colorful wall hangings out of yarn.

I make little kits for the car. A kit for napkins and plastic forks. A kit for diapers, and bibs, and burp clothes.

When I have exhausted every possible chore, I sort through the gift-wrapping tissue I've saved, and color coordinate it. I admire the vibrant box when I've finished and think—

She is in all of this.

My mother.

Sorting through little boxes and papers all day long. Crafting my favorite velvet vest with sparkling embellishments when I was eight and sewing my Halloween costumes late into the night.

She is in me—myself as mother, large and waiting—putting navy blue and pink and yellow tissues in their place.

She told me how she too was pregnant. She said it was her ex-husband's and had her cervix checked that afternoon. She also asked me how my brother Paul felt about being the father of my child.

I watched our corn growing as she spoke. Realized how much better it was doing this year. The sunflowers were much taller too.

She paused often with confusion, tripping over the names of all the men who had left her.

"I went to the old house," she said. "Bob was there. I mean Paul. No Dan, er…Ed. Bob. Bob was there and he rubbed my belly, which felt so good. And I realized *Oh, God, no! This isn't a baby. It's not a baby. It's pain.*"

I watched the ants marching and working hard along the cracked bricks under my feet. There was no reasonable point to interrupt her, so I said, "Mom, B's calling me in for dinner."

She said, "Oh ok," and told me that she hoped I would tell her if my brother was really the father.

The trellis was full and green. She'd be so impressed with our grapevines this year. It was dreamy—the way we snacked off them while watering the grass.

On July 30, 2017, our daughter is born—fifteen days overdue. We name her Poppy.

Everything else waits. The yard is set aside, and the weeds grow thick. The grapes turn to raisins and litter the grass. The strawberries shrink. The sweet potato plants grow hearty without us noticing. The lemon tree is exploding.

The grass is now dirt and our dog, Harjo, whines as I sit on the couch nursing Poppy all day long.

Motherhood is so hard. And labor was so hard. I wish more women had told me.

On the third day I cry softly and wonder how long I will be hostage to the sofa.

The mornings are nice. I stay in bed with her while she nurses and I drink coffee and play music and take photos.

She is so tiny.

With a crazed animal kind of love, I clench my teeth every time I pick her up.

I am so torn up down there and swear I will never do this again.

I am always scared now, and I wonder every day how on earth my mother did it on her own.

When Poppy was born, she had my mother's fingernails. All of them, witchy.

The top of her head had the sweetest smell.

How do I explain the scent of warmth?

Warm roses

Warm vanilla

Warm breath

Warm chocolate

Her head and her soft belly, untouched and ivory.

Her face like no other. Everything warm.

But my mother was in there no doubt.

This woman was ours.

Poppy is six months old. She and I are up at six a.m. I open the blinds in the living room even though it is still dark. At seven, the sun will rise and turn the mountains pink and we don't like to miss it. In the mornings I lay her on the bathmat while I pee and brush my teeth. She looks at me from upside down and smiles. She always smiles.

I make her a bottle with one hand and set her in her swing. She eagerly takes the bottle and sucks hard. Then I make coffee and do whatever chore I can accomplish before the bottle is finished.

We've been in the house seven days. Every morning is the same. Quiet and dark and sweet.

But this morning my phone rings at six-thirty.

Minneapolis.

I wait for the voicemail.

I had read before the feeling a person has when their parent dies—like being punched in the stomach. And the achy sick feeling just resides there, pulsating.

The first day was the longest.

On the first day I felt no shock or denial. I felt her death inside of me. I knew to cry.

B built a fire and gathered enough wood to last a full day. The house and its surroundings wrapped me up as I grieved. The sun didn't get too bright. The cows were quiet. The wood burned extra long.

When I wasn't crying I'd sit still, facing our large living room window and made odd expressions as I watched the turkey vultures sitting on their posts patiently, and the blue jays swoop past me playfully, and the image of her falling again and again and again.

And every so often I'd mutter a name under my breath who should know of her passing.

"Mary-Lee."

"Mike Clemming."

"Ed."

"My dad."

Behind my grief were those not grieving. My father-in-law kept his distance. My mother-in-law brought frozen chicken potpies and told me an odd story of how her aunt had been murdered. B held Poppy. The dog played in the yard and came inside smelling of rosemary.

My sister's seven-year-old triplets don't like the photos of my mother from when she was healthy.

"That's not Gramma," they say, pointing to a healthy, slightly overweight woman.

"*That's* Gramma," and point to a recent photo of her: thin, sick, and unbearably small.

"Well, you know, guys, that's not the mom I'll remember. Grandma used to be a lot less fragile."

"*NOOOOOO*," they all protest.

I show them her senior portrait from college. "See? She used to be young and healthy like me."

"I hate that picture," Fletcher yells.

"How did Gramma die?" Finn asks.

"She fell down," I tell them.

"I don't believe you," he says. "No one dies from falling."

"You do when you're very fragile."

"No, Ash-i-ley, I don't believe you." I don't believe it either.

Fletcher is standing in the kitchen and says, "Yes, Finn, I'll show you. She fell like this…" and proceeds to twirl around in a half circle and fall to the ground on his stomach. He lies there a moment and I'm surprised to see how accurate his body looks to what I imagined.

"Stop you guys," Abby whines. "You'll make Ash-i-ley cry."

I looked through everything. When I felt I had gone through it all, I went through it again. It didn't take long enough. The men from before had taken most of it, after all. She lost it all and what she kept was meager—for a hoarder anyway.

I checked the microwave for a forgotten coffee mug but there wasn't one. I looked through her sock drawer and pulled out a pair of soft lounge socks and a pair of white ones with gold embroidered anchors sewn into the cuffs and kept them because I remembered them on her so clearly.

I opened two large trunks to find her favorite sweaters wrapped in plastic bags. I felt giddy as I pulled them out one-by-one, remembering them well.

I tried them on. Rhinestones, sequins, shoulder pads and fur. I found a pleather tube top with matching skirt and held it up to myself in the mirror, remembering it as one of her "ladies' night" outfits. I picked out a few of my favorite sweaters, sprayed them heavily with her perfume and put them in a duffle bag.

I kept tripping on her wheelchair as I moved about and felt compelled to apologize as if she were sitting there, watching me.

In the closet hung the fur coat she'd wrap around me for our long trips to Monmouth when the heat was out.

In her purse I found little papers, hand sanitizer, and a pink lipstick in a pink beaded compact. I put the lipstick on.

On the window ledge were the heart-shaped rocks I had brought her the year before, all spread out thoughtfully. Next to them were my Swarvorski crystals I collected as a child. I exhaled with a sob, picking them up one at a time, overwhelmed with nostalgia. I inspected them against the light, remembering how I'd dust each one carefully with the tip of a rag. I wrapped them in bubble wrap and put them in the bag too.

A loud humming sound suddenly filled the room and I realized it was the radiator by the window. It read seventy-one degrees and buzzed lightly for a minute or two. Of course, the room was heated but it felt like an intrusion or a mockery. I wanted to tell it to fuck off—that there wasn't anyone to keep warm. And then I wondered how many times it had gone off the night she died.

I looked through the bathroom cupboards and drawers. She had taken every last toiletry from the townhouse. I picked up deodorants I recognized from high school and checked the expiration. Sure enough: 2002. I opened empty compacts of Mary Kay makeup and sprayed her perfume in the air.

On the bathroom counter I found her emergency call button in a sunglass case. Puzzled, I held it and wondered why it was here and not next to her bed. I imagined that she had forgotten it there before bed and had no way of calling for help after she fell.

"I'm no expert," the funeral director had said, "but it's my opinion that Donna was dead before she hit the floor." I hated the way he said that.

I would've liked to believe it, but I wasn't convinced. I held the pager tight in my hand wondering if it was the last thing my mother longed for.

I went to the closet and pulled out the large fur coat. I laid down on the bed next to all the tiny papers and pulled it over me, the thick fur collar around my neck, and wept.

"We'll go in together," he told me.

I put my arm into his. He wore a bright blue dress shirt. The same one he wore to my real wedding.

Katie had already gone in to see her. She flew past me, dramatically, said, "Don't go in there."

Even in this perfectly acceptable time to be dramatic, her reaction bothered me.

We walked into the chapel and I saw just the top of my mother's forehead and the tip of her nose poking out of the casket. I stopped but my brother kept walking ahead of me. I followed slowly but couldn't move any closer once her face was in view.

I watched him glide toward her as if he were floating. Without hesitation he picked a red rose from one of the bouquets and placed it in her hands, casually, as if he were giving a flower to someone he adored. He then laid each hand on her casket, bent his head, exhaled and turned to walk back towards me.

I just stood there, with envy of his courage and suave. And then he hugged me, and I sobbed into his chest.

"That's not her," he said.

And I knew that. But still I cried.

I sobbed out of fear. My denial had brought her back to life, so then, what was this thing—this taxidermy lookalike, all painted and hairsprayed and naked from the waist down? I feared her like I would a monster or villain in a movie who was pretending to be dead only to grab my wrist when I got too close.

I couldn't tell you the rings she wore. Or the earrings. I only remember what looked wrong. Her mouth in a straight line, no doubt, stitched to upturn the frown she wore in her sleep. The shape of her nose—skeletal and sunken "from the dying tissue in her cheeks," Boyfriend of twenty-five years casually told me. The soft pink sweater I clutched as she walked me down the aisle a year prior. The realization that the last thing she saw me in was a white wedding gown, and there I stood in a black dress.

I forgot how death deflates the hands.

I couldn't say goodbye.

I could feel her disappointment, and still, I felt myself recoil further away from her like I might if she were alive and hugging me for too long and too tightly.

Her name was displayed on a large screen above the podium with a tacky beach scene chosen (by whom?) from some insignificant library of graphics.

My throat was dry. Poppy was quiet in her stroller.

I just wanted to go home.

I just wanted everyone to stop talking to me.

To be quiet.

We used to come to this church for Christmas Eve service when I was little. Actually my mother normally fell asleep on the couch before we'd make it out the door and would get upset with me and Boyfriend of however many years for not waking her up.

It looks the same. I fucking hate it here.

Everyone is singing badly to hymns I've never heard.

The whiskey is hot in my belly, thank God.

Minnesota 2000-2012

When her thighs were large, and her face was tan in the summer.

When she still worried about losing weight.

When we fought a lot. Like when I straightened my hair too much before my senior photo shoot.

And when she brought too many pairs of black shoes to Monmouth for her mother's funeral and the car was already so fucking packed.

When I had plans to leave.

When I made plans so I could cut our visits short.

When everything about her drove me crazy.

And when everything important lay ahead.

The Friday before you arrive is windy. Off Highway 1, an egret hangs in the air, awkwardly soaring with crooked legs.

I sleep hard and dream of you a little.

The next morning the post office calls to tell me you arrived, so I pick you up on my way to work.

You weigh one pound, thirteen ounces. The same size as a quart of blueberries.

I put you on the floorboard of the passenger seat. I speak to you a little.

"So here you are…I'm going to try to keep my shit together right now. I guess you're coming to work with me."

CREMATED REMAINS stickers cover the box.

"It's a really pretty drive," I say. "You'll get to hang out in a vineyard today. And hey, if you're with me right now, maybe you could keep this Pandora station going? I don't get any service out here."

Every song plays without pause.

At work I imagine you walking through the vineyard, smelling the air, petting the sheep. Embracing a place you've never been. Embracing a you you've never been.

On our way home, magpies play in the road.

"Those are magpies, Mom. And those are olive trees." I imagine you telling me to slow down.

At home I hold Poppy. She stares at my red eyes and smells mysteriously of Fruit Loops. Outside, the ranchers are rounding up and branding the cattle. B builds a fire before the sun goes down. I put another log on while he puts Poppy to bed and watch the ashes float like static.

Your box is covered in tape. After only a few cuts, the cardboard flap flips open. Inside you're covered in bubble wrap. And beneath all that is a white plastic box with a gold label:

CREMATED REMAINS OF
DONNA ELAINE WARREN
#057694

It's warm in my hands, and weighty. Like you're alive.

I open it slightly. It makes a pop as I lift the cap and I look inside just long enough to glimpse your remains, which I can tell right away are nothing like ashes.

I imagine pouring you into the vase like a bag of flour, spilling clumsily and crying. So I close you back up.

My eyes are hot and heavy. I feel exhausted like I did at your funeral. Like I did at my wedding. Like I did after giving birth. Like I did after a long day at the amusement park when I was little, nodding off in the back seat on the car ride home.

fiction

This Be the Verse

anna winham

I wasn't looking for a diagnosis, exactly. I had already combed through the DSM, three different editions actually, a few years ago for a final project. Adjacent to the project itself, I'd determined that I exhibited a number of behaviours that correlated with certain entries, even if they didn't fully qualify me for any particular condition.

I didn't put too much stock in these definitions anyway. I viewed myself as OCD-*leaning*. Not in a hygienic way, as any of my friends would leap to tell you. But in a "my clothing must be organised precisely by garment length, sleeve length, collar type, colour, and fabric weight" kind of way. Shoes by staff height, heel height, amount of foot covering, material, and colour. Books by genre, topic, author, and date of acquisition. People by height, weight, gender, and topics of interest.

Similarly, I considered myself *prone* to eating disorders, though I hadn't had one. I always made sure to consume at least 1560 calories per day, since this is the SAT score over which it makes statistically no difference whether one will get into Harvard or not. And after noticing that I catastrophised almost as much as I fantasised, I considered that I might have a mild case of generalised anxiety disorder. This wasn't something that particularly distressed me, just something that I noted.

In any case, I ended up with a therapist. I will not tell you her name. I did not know very much about her, but her name is one of the things that I knew. I wasn't sure why I was going to therapy, some vague sense that my life could be improved and that possibly therapy might be one thing that could improve it. The same way eating more kale or trying a Bellini for the first time might improve one's life, but also might not. In this sense therapy seemed worth a shot. A kind of expensive shot, but for life improvement why not?

I had come to suspect, however, that the therapy was not improving my life. I couldn't tell you for sure if my life was better or worse than it would have been if not for the therapy, not having the benefit of counter-factuals in real life. The only thing I could tell you was that for two days prior to my sessions I traipsed through my life with dread in my heart, rehearsing what I would say to the therapist.

Whenever I was fighting with my boyfriend, I made sure to make up on Tuesday evening so that by Wednesday morning I could tell the therapist that my relationship was going well. I quit drinking on weekdays so as not to be hungover when meeting the therapist. I added thirty minutes of light aerobics to my exercise routine three days a week so I could prove to the therapist that I had a healthy and non-obsessive relationship with both food and my body. In case she ever brought that up.

A few weeks into therapy I set a recurring Sunday afternoon alarm to remind me to speak with my sister. If the therapist asked who had called whom I could answer proudly that I had been the one to reach out, demonstrating my clear position as the mature and open sibling of the family.

The therapist would ask me questions like, "and how did you feel about that?" and whenever I would say, "angry," or, "nothing," or, "satisfied," she would say, "and what was behind that anger?" and I soon learned that if I said "sadness," she herself would be satisfied. My therapist felt I was emotionally detached.

The therapist would often tell me that if anything happened, I could always call her. I suppose this was nice of her, but I wondered what she thought might happen and why I would call her if it did. I had told the therapist that I had a broad set of friends with whom I had loving and fulfilling relationships. When I went to stay with my mum and dad during a global pandemic, my therapist appeared concerned, "will you be okay?" I had managed to survive twenty-six years with my parents so far. I assured the therapist that I would indeed be okay.

The therapist thought I had a low bar for *okay*. When pushed, I defined *okay* as *surviving*, and even though I clarified that this was not my preferred state, I would be okay if I had to survive for a while. I really had to spend a lot of time reassuring the therapist.

I would leave the sessions feeling dehydrated. Not from crying, which I didn't do, which seemed to upset the therapist, who asked if I was holding back my emotions. I had asked the therapist if she wished for me to produce the depths of my despair on cue. She seemed alarmed by my use of the word "despair." I instead felt dehydrated because I usually imbibe a steady stream of tap water, but the therapist seemed to think my frequent sips were some kind of distraction from my feelings.

The therapist would ask me what I was hoping to gain from going to therapy, and I could only reply that I wasn't sure, as I had no context for this one-on-one paid social interaction, having never undergone the procedure previously. Some friends had recommended it and being an open-minded sort of individual, I had decided to try it out. My therapist suggested that perhaps I was not so open-minded.

One day it dawned on me that I had better demonstrate my great emotional depth to my therapist. If only she *knew* how deeply it upset me to see her so clearly frustrated by my so-called repression. Or that it *so* gratified me when, upon my reply of "sadness?" she would smile knowingly, lean back in her soft leather chair, her crow's feet crinkling behind her striking gold-rimmed eyeglasses, and nod.

"Yes, sadness," she would say softly, like I was a dim child and it was our secret. I thought that if only we could have a few more of those moments then the therapy might work a bit better. This was certainly within my control.

I began orchestrating emotional dramas for our discussions. I thought it would be easier to demonstrate depth if we had some good material to work with. I began with little things. When they had run out of tofu scallion cream cheese at the bagel place where I would stop on the way to our sessions, I saw a golden opportunity. This was really not a huge deal as they did still have tofu *vegetable* cream cheese, but I instead asked to speak to the manager and gave him a piece of my mind.

"Just what do you expect the vegans who are also deathly allergic to red peppers to eat?" I railed.

"I'm so sorry," said the nice bald man who often mistakenly called me Molly, "I didn't realise you had an allergy."

"I don't," I stormed, "but someone might!"

They gave me my order for free. I was a regular there, and they must have just assumed I was having a bad day. But I was having a brilliant day. I got to tell my therapist all about the incident. When I'd finished telling her about the cream cheese, she said, "and what was behind all that anger?"

And I said, "sadness. Sadness! SADNESS!"

She leaned back in her chair in that satisfying way of hers.

Instead of resolving my next fight with dear Joseph, I escalated it. It began innocuously, as most fights between ultimately loving couples do. He fell asleep while we were watching *Fantastic Fungi*, if you can believe that, and while this was a trait I would usually find endearing, I knew I could make my mark. I nudged him awake roughly, elbow-forward. Eyes half-shut, he mumbled to himself, moving towards me for a kiss, but I resisted the obviously adorable nature of a grown man drooling and I snapped!

"You don't care about me!" Oh, we had a great fight. I dropped several plates on the ground and the neighbours banged on the apartment wall.

I ended up leaving in the middle of the night, passive-aggressively Venmo-charging him for the car service I took to my own apartment, naming the charge "the money I could have spent with LITERALLY ANYONE ELSE."

The next morning in therapy we had a good chat about attachment styles, the importance of staying put during a discussion about one's relationship, the nature of my relationship with my father, the whole nine yards. I considered actually telling her about my mum, who was dead now, but it didn't seem relevant. And besides, she didn't ask.

Naturally with this success under my belt, I wanted to step up my game. Till this point I had got on pretty well with my roommate, who was a high school friend of a college friend of mine. We were just friendly enough that it was nice to live with her but not such good friends that we felt obliged to spend all our time together. Anyway, that relationship had to go. I poisoned her cat and she said I was insane and called our mutual friend who also said I was insane and had to move out *immediately*. Which I did.

This provided a lot of rich material for therapy—how angry must I have been to kill the cat? And how much sadness behind the anger! Possibly even verging on the much anticipated "despair." When I mentioned that my roommate was really sad about the cat, the therapist asked me how I felt about that. I was tempted to say that I thought this was a reasonable emotional reaction, but by this time I knew that the therapist would say, "but how do *you* feel, Emma?" and so I simply said, "oh, very sad."

The therapist actually said if it seemed like I was going to do anything like that again she would have to call the police, so I knew we were getting somewhere.

Since things were going so well, I decided to discuss a piece of my writing with my therapist. I was excited that it had been accepted for publication in a religious studies journal. I was not particularly religious myself, not even spiritual, I had told the therapist, who it turned out believed in "energy," which in a sense I did too. But I did have an active interest in enough questions that I usually found myself surrounded by fanatics, I assured her. The piece in question detailed a series of attempts to communicate something, but the thing proved slippery in the telling. It was a meditation, I had told her, on whether it was ultimately possible to tell the truth. You know, given the limitations of language, perception, and whatnot. The therapist told me I just had to tell my truth.

winham

At this point I realised the therapy may be bad for my work.

All in all, the two days of crippling foreboding coupled with the twelve-hour hangover from repeating "sadness…sadness…sadness" forty-five times in forty-five minutes led me to suspect that this practice was not worth either the time or money that it took up.

This is not to say that I was happy or well-adjusted in any sense. Indeed, I was most likely deeply unhappy. It did appear that I was what one might call "stable" or "coping very well." Friends had called me these specific things, in fact, before therapy.

I ditched the therapist in an email. After all, we had a professional relationship, even if her profession was highly personal. I told her I had spoken to a couple of friends and wanted to thank her for helping me to realise that I did not need a therapist after all. I worried that she would think I was running away from the important emotional confrontations she was bringing to the fore weekly. Then I thought, I can send one email and cease forever henceforth worrying about what my therapist thinks of me.

I do still worry about my therapist. Her open-minded ways, her lack of concern about the nature of truth. But since there are no counter-factuals in real life, I know there's no way for me to know whether I would worry more or less if I had either never seen her or never stopped seeing her. And there's certainly no use worrying about that.

Skeleton

gogo zoger

In my body
a knocking goes
door-to-door.
Stopping at each bone,

every cooled, hollow vessel
left emptied of warm emblems- glowing light.

It pries stories
from my clenched jaw-
bites at my fucking toes.

Pulling at me heavy,
my body lays,

crumpled over at the waist
blood-
filling up at the face.

What once sprung from floor boards,
sitting ripe, propped up from its grave; Your Face appears,

without warning you make your way across the room,
melting our souls to heartbreak soup.

Seasoned lightly.
Hot to the touch.

I blow gently-
steam cutting sharp
as it swirls away.

Sleeping now
as if innocence could
fill
the body,
grace my skull.

nonfiction

My Own Terms
andrew stevens

Content warning for suicide.

"Based on these test results, you're going to kill yourself *yesterday*," a therapist once said to me, eager to hear some explanation that might satiate his inclination to commit me. I just told him that the diagnostic exam, which would directly ascribe words like "depression" and "anxiety disorder" to me for the first time, wasn't specific about how recently or regularly I'd felt suicidal.

Growing up, I was certain there was no way I'd make it past eighteen. I was so wholly consumed with the thought of ending my life that any other outcome was a pipe dream. Reaching my twenties was as likely as being the first man on Mars. I'd set trivial timelines for myself: *If things don't get better by the end of this year, I'm out.*

When I started drinking and started fucking, I realized that I could at least commit myself to sticking around long enough to continue doing both of those things, the hedonistic pleasure providing some of the connection I was sorely lacking in my childhood.

But building up that initial thought process in my developmental years left cigarette burns on my brain. I'm twenty-nine now, and I still can't envision my future—long-term life goals have always remained just outside my reach. Folks ask where I see myself in five years, and I fall back to being that fifteen-year-old featherweight who never imagined an answer beyond total blackness.

Yet, when you've dealt with suicidal ideation as long as I have, daydreams of dalliances with death become mundane. "I should kill myself" pops into my head as casually as "I'm hungry." Often, it's reactionary—an inherent inclination to end it all after the many instances of my regrettable behavior begin to reverberate around my brain. I'll remember that I kissed my friend's girlfriend, or a moment of inebriated oversharing, or all the thirsty unanswered texts I've sent, or another of my endless other rejections, mistakes, and failures, and my cringe creeps toward a clear-cut kamikaze solution.

The banality of it all hardly makes the harshest moments any easier, however. When my sources of serotonin and dopamine are desperately depleted, I'm plagued by more specific thoughts telling me to dive through one of the plate-glass windows in the office and plummet from the eighteenth floor, to not bother looking both ways before walking into traffic, to swallow every pill I can find in the house. *Just fucking do it. You're worthless and no one will miss you*, my depression sometimes screams at me, as I puff on purple haze to impermanently purge my mind of thoughts entirely.

I still think about my own death as often as I did when I was fifteen, so much that I'm not sure I fear it anymore, at least not as much as you're supposed to. I'm far more terrified by the thought of growing old and losing my mind completely. As I've told therapists in recent history, the primary difference between fifteen and now is that now I know I'm not going to kill myself.

But even that's only a half-truth: I'm not actively planning some grand suicide, certainly not while my mother and my cat still live and breathe, but I still can't imagine going out on any terms other than my own. If senility starts to set in or cancer points its grisly face my way, I want to be the one that makes the decision, be it by bullet or pulling the plug. I need that; it's my only true escape.

To me, continuing to live with disease and dementia would be a choice—and not one I plan to make, my survival instinct sorely lacking as it is. My death may be an inevitability, but I intend to have a say in its deliverance.

The Parent

charlie j. stephens

Once a month Greta and I have dinner with Katie and Chloe, a couple who have been friends with Greta since long before I met her. They're my *inherited friends*, I like to call them. We usually go out for an over-priced dinner—New American with craft cocktails, talk about the kids, tell stories from work, then hug and walk away. Immediately after each of these occasions, I vow never to do it again.

"How many couple-selfies do two people need to take at an hour-long dinner?" I asked Greta, after our last double date.

She can't go along with my complaints though; she and Chloe have been through a lot as friends, and Greta is fiercely loyal.

"She just really likes to document and remember the fun moments," Greta explained.

I started in on another way to criticize Katie and Chloe but stopped myself, because I love Greta and really do try not to be a jerk.

"Well, she may or may not remember the four whiskey sours she just downed," I joked, and got a little laugh out of Greta. She is loyal but she can still see the humor in things.

"You're a real asshole," she said to me, grabbing her keys on the way out the door and kissing me on the neck.

I love that about Greta: the easy, irreverent way she handles things. You can bet the next day pictures of Katie and Chloe were mood-lighting-filtered to perfection, and posted all over social media, along with some picture of their gorgeous sixteen-year-old son, Etienne, doing something impressive, like winning the latest cross-country competition, blond curls flying, or counting out all his internship money to donate to a local charity.

Our son Jayden is a teenager also, but no one even remotely prepared me for what a repellant human being he would become. Jayden is seventeen and has *anger management issues* but that is putting it lightly. *Overwhelming hostility and violent tendencies* might paint a more accurate picture. He's worse than ever these days, but the thing is, there's always been something wrong with him, all the way back to when he was a toddler. All I know for sure—more than anything else—is I'm not a person who is cut out for raising anyone.

"Stay the fuck out of my room you fucking cunt hole" is a phrase I recently heard yelled down our very own hallway.

We took away all his privileges for that, but what else can you do? At age seventeen he towers over us at 5'11" and seems to be growing a faint but unnerving moustache. Whenever he wears shorts, I am still shocked by his dark, hairy legs. His bedroom walls are decorated with fist-sized craters and his window is cracked. I think he hit it with one of the Nerf guns he's had since he was nine and still refuses to get rid of, even though he'll be a senior next year. I offered him twenty bucks to take all the guns to Goodwill last weekend and he rolled his eyes and said, "You don't understand me at all."

He has a point. I've always harbored a fear Jayden will grow up to be schizophrenic or an arsonist, maybe both. He has night terrors when he's sick where he sees demons coming towards him, and he's been trying to burn things up since he first learned the word "hot." We have him in therapy but he refuses to talk to his therapist. Week after week, another $150 goes down the drain, as the therapist reports back, "No he didn't share anything this time," but that he was willing to listen to a calming whale song recording for thirty minutes.

"Isn't it ironic that Jayden's therapy sessions make me want to kill myself?" I ask Greta.

"It'll be okay," she tells me and pats my shoulder, no longer willing to engage with me on the tired subject of my pessimism about Jayden. After so many years—years that, overall, I would categorize as nightmarish, Greta has somehow managed to hold out this steady well-spring of hope for him, and it's the aspect of our relationship that causes the greatest rift between us. She's stayed right there with him—the time in 5th grade he called one of his teachers a "dirty whore" in class, and when he slammed our dog's head in the door and showed no remorse. There was also the time he set fire to the wooden swing set in our neighbor's backyard. And so many more incidents. I really can't imagine how it's possible he could turn out okay, but Greta has this intense trust in him, in her parenting process, and in some future result that she alone can see.

Tonight, we are meeting Katie and Chloe for dinner again, and I'm already dreading it. What really gets me is how they go on and on, all the time about how they're so queer. I guess anyone can say that these days, and I don't want to police anyone, but from my view, they are so blatantly normal, even the straightest straight people in the world seem more interesting to me in comparison. They had a traditional wedding with about a million people, and required matching bridesmaid dresses from a cheap, taffeta emporium based in San Lorenzo. The worst part is they're constantly touching each other at dinner, as though they can't keep their hands off each other when I know, for a fact, they haven't had sex in over a year.

As for my other pet-peeve, you can be guaranteed to get a card with the cutest pictures of Katie and Chloe, and Etienne of course, every year at Christmas. You know they had to go through thousands of images because they self-document every damn minute. The process must take days, maybe weeks. Greta puts the annual card on the fridge when it arrives in the mail, and it's the only time I feel glad my only child might grow up to be a schizophrenic arsonist, because at least that's interesting.

"Do we really need to put it up again this year?" I ask Greta.

"If they come over, they might wonder where it is. Besides, I kind of like it. They spend a lot of time together as a family. I think it's sweet." She looks at me, probably wondering if I'll finally see them from her perspective, but I just can't.

"What if we make a holiday card, print it on gorgeous paper and send it out with some gold envelopes, but the only pictures will be of Jayden bathed in computer light playing violent video games with his usual disturbed grimace?"

"You're absolutely impossible," she says.

The dinner place Katie and Chloe choose tonight is a hipster eatery where everyone working looks to be about twelve years old. I make the mistake, after appetizers and against my own instincts, of telling Katie and Chloe how much I have been struggling with Jayden since we saw them last. I usually try not to talk with them about parenting issues because it just makes me feel worse to divulge anything vulnerable to them. I'm not sure what compels me to share this time; maybe it's just been an extremely hard week, and I can't hold it in anymore. I keep thinking things can't get any worse, but time after time, something else Jayden does sends me off the deep end. I tell them what happened last weekend.

"Jayden started a YouTube channel and I found it online. It's about how America's biggest problem is that women keep falsely accusing men of rape, and how girls at his school treat him like shit." I watch their faces. "I'm seriously afraid he's on the path to becoming an incel."

They look back at me with a profound inability to relate, but after a short silence, recover quickly enough to offer some advice.

"What we do," Katie explains in a voice laden with earnestness, "is read a selection of poetry from the book *Gratitude Here and Now* before we sit down to eat dinner. It might help Jayden feel more grounded. I have an extra copy if you want to borrow it."

But all I want to do is stab her with my salad fork, and I feel an over-whelming jolt of compassion for Jayden.

God, he must feel like this all the time, I think.

"Etienne just loves it," Chloe chimes in.

Something deep in me snaps completely then, and I can't tolerate being pleasant anymore. I don't want to be polite, or suffer through their superficial groping, and I most definitely do not want to borrow *Gratitude Here and Now*. I don't know where this is going, but I burst out laughing like a lunatic, the kind of laughter that only gets worse when you try to tamp it down, and then I'm talking to them in a clear, low voice that doesn't even sound like mine.

"Are you fucking serious?" I ask, and Greta gives me a cautionary, terrified look. "You don't get it—or us—at all. Jayden would brutally murder both of us on the spot with the nearest butter knife if we tried to read any Rumi or whatnot to him at dinnertime. And the thing is, I wouldn't blame him. Etienne is boring as fuck. Your marriage is boring as fuck. And these dinners are boring as fuck."

No one is laughing now, not even me. No, I am definitely not laughing anymore. I look at their shocked faces, and worry I've finally ruined everything with Greta, and wonder how or if she will forgive me. But in that moment, all I want to do is find Jayden, and tell him how much he means to me. Maybe I can get him to go for a drive with me, fast on the highway like he likes. I want him to understand that I finally understand something that he understands. I am hellbent on conveying this to him.

I walk out of the restaurant, and pull up my collar to the night air—letting myself believe for this one moment—that maybe redemption is only possible when, like Jayden, we send it all up in a blaze, and see who is still there beside us when the ashes settle.

poem

The Unsaid

lois rosen

You never told him
you ended it
because of his many little hairs
edging the bathroom sink
brown scum
around the rim

and because he
started blacking dates
on your calendar, marking
in a month of him

Whoa
you should have said

Instead
you traveled with him
all the way from Salem
to Seattle's Folklife Festival
then insisted he sleep
in the second of
the motel room's double beds

At Scottish Music
you left him with
the tartan-clad dancers'
tricky formations
and bagpipes

while you marched
past the parade
of giant-size puppets
papier-mâché heads
towering above you

spooned cobbler
syrupy berries
and dollop after dollop
of whipped cream
into your stuffed
and smeary mouth

Baggage
melissa siig

My father's move away from us was like a train pulling out of the station—it started out slow, then gradually picked up steam. He first moved into an apartment at the bottom of our street. We could walk there in twenty minutes. It had tennis courts and a beautiful neighbor, a Norwegian divorcee named Caryn, seven years older than him. They quickly started dating.

My sisters spent the night at my father's apartment every weekend. I, however, have no memory of ever staying there. As a thirteen-year-old, I must had been too busy with friends, or simply refused. But I do remember his refrigerator. It didn't have much in it except for his staples—cottage cheese, tomatoes, cucumbers, yellow cheese, eggs, buttermilk. But the freezer. The freezer was overflowing with ice-cream sandwiches. He would stock up on them whenever 7-11 was having a sale.

Every other Thursday was also his night with us, and he would take us to McDonald's. My father loved McDonald's. It was fast and cheap and tasted good, and he thought it was the best bang for your buck. After he moved back to Israel, whenever he came to visit us in the States one of the first things he did was go to McDonald's. There were no McDonald's in Israel yet, only McDavid's, a kosher copycat of the Golden Arches that was nowhere near as tasty. Plus, since it was kosher, it did not have cheeseburgers.

My father truly believed that McDonald's was good for you.

"You know, Melissa," he would say, "you can't find better soft-serve than McDonald's. As long as I eat my fruits and take my walks, I can eat McDonald's every day. It's perfectly healthy. What? You don't believe me?"

My father ate vegetables and fruit every day. An orange was his favorite after-dinner dessert. He would even eat the inside of the peel, scraping the white meat with his teeth like he was munching on corn-on-the-cob. When a boy I was dating in seventh grade asked if he could come over to our house, my father—who was out of oranges—said yes, but only if he brought him an orange. To my embarrassment, the boy showed up on our doorstep with his outstretched hand holding an orange like a peace offering.

One Saturday morning at home (my mother's house would always be my home) I came upstairs to find my ten-year-old sister, Julie, in her pajamas curled up on the couch watching cartoons. My baby sister, Anna, was asleep next to her in the pack n' play.

"What are you doing here?" I asked. Julie's blond hair was a mess and she was clutching her Dada, the security blanket that she had since birth. The blanket had started out its life cream-colored but with love and the passage of years it had turned a dingy gray. The satin trim had been rubbed between her fingers so many times it was now almost all but gone, the edges frayed like tassels on a leather jacket. "I thought you slept at Dad's last night."

"We did sleep there, but I woke up in the middle of the night to Anna crying and I couldn't find Daddy, so I called Mommy."

"What do you mean you couldn't find Daddy?" I asked. Anna stirred in the pack n' play, her little fists opening and closing like she was grasping for something, but she didn't wake up. An empty bottle lay in a corner. She had probably thrown it there when she had finished all the milk.

"He wasn't in his room. He wasn't anywhere in the apartment."

"Where was he? He left you all alone?"

Julie didn't take her eyes off the TV. She was watching *Inspector Gadget*.

"I didn't know where he was."

I leaned against the doorway to the den. I felt guilty that I hadn't been there.

"So, what did you do?"

"I got Anna out of her crib and went upstairs and called Mommy, and she came and got us." A commercial came on and Julie finally looked at me. "It was scary."

I heard the schussing of my mom's slippers as she walked down the hallway towards the den. She was wrapped up in her robe, her hands hiding in the pockets.

"Turns out he was at Caryn's," she said, shaking her head and rubbing her eyes. She looked tired. "Oh, he got an earful from me."

Gradually, my dad started moving farther away from us. He took an apartment at the end of town—one we could no longer walk to. One day, Anna, only two years old, flushed his car keys down the toilet. My father was furious. I think she was trying to get him to stay. But it didn't work. A year after my parent's "temporary" separation, I came home from high school to find my father sitting at our kitchen counter.

"I have something to tell you," he said.

I opened the freezer and pulled out a carton of Ben N' Jerry's ice cream. I sensed he had something important to say to me and I knew it was going to gut me. I didn't look at him while I scooped the ice cream into a bowl. I would not help him get the words out that were going to cause me pain. I would not be an accomplice in my demise.

"I am moving back to Israel," he said calmly. "I am going to try it for one year."

There. He had done it. He had thrown the knife into my core and twisted it. But I would not let him see my pain. I would not let him know that I cared.

"I knew you would," was all I said, and took my bowl of ice cream into the den to watch *Days of Our Lives* as if my father had just told me he had canceled our date at McDonald's that night.

I would regret my response for decades to come. With the wisdom of adulthood, I see my retort as that of a child protecting herself from devastating news, but for many years I blamed myself for everything that followed. If only I had said something different, something more loving or heart wrenching, I could have stopped him from leaving. If only I had said, "No Daddy, don't go," and fallen into his arms crying, maybe he wouldn't have left. But I was fourteen and too aloof and absorbed in my teenage world to say anything like that. The guilt stayed with me, hiding under my scalp like a seed waiting to bloom. When I finally shared these feelings with my mother when I was in my thirties, she told me I was ridiculous.

"You were the child, Melissa. He was the adult," she said. "He had already made up his mind. You could never have stopped him from leaving."

My parents have different stories about my father's decision to move back to his homeland. They both start with my father visiting his family in Jerusalem for a Passover seder, but there the stories diverge. My mother recounts how, upon his return to San Francisco, he showed up unexpectedly at the beauty shop while she was getting her hair colored. He said they needed to talk.

They went to a nearby café, where my father broke the news.

"I am leaving," he told her. "I am moving back to Israel. I can't do it here. I can't make a living. I can't make it work."

My father had been a stockbroker since we moved to the Bay Area in 1981, but towards the end of my parent's marriage he decided—without ever having gone to law school in America—that he wanted to be a lawyer again. He had a law degree from Hebrew University in Jerusalem, but to practice law in San Francisco he needed to pass the notoriously difficult California BAR exam. He took, and failed, the exam nine times. Each time he retook the test, I would make a bargain with God as I walked home from school. I would pick a leaf from a bush and if it came off whole, he would pass the test. Obviously, God did not like my deal.

When my father finally tired from relentless studying and retaking of the BAR, he settled on trying his hand at being a real estate agent. He passed that test, but I don't remember if he sold a single house.

After the beauty shop, my father took my mother out to coffee. She was hysterical.

"How can you do this? How can you leave your three girls? How can you leave me to raise them on my own?" she pleaded with my father. But in his mind, he was already packing his bags. Nothing could persuade him to stay.

My father's account was much simpler. He moved back to Jerusalem for love. In his recounting, he returned to Israel to visit his family for three weeks for Passover, ran into an old girlfriend from elementary school with doe-like brown eyes and a body my father later proudly described as *zaftik*, the Yiddish word for voluptuous. He fell in love with Anat and left his three children to move halfway across the world to be with her. He shared none of this with us at the time.

My father was going to miss Anna's entire childhood. And he did. She has no recollection of what it was like to have a father who lived in the same house, or even in the same town, as her. I often wondered which is more painful—to never have had a father in the truest sense of the word, or to have had one, a good one, and suffered the pain of losing him. It was when I thought of my father that I completely disagreed with Alfred Lord Tennyson's famous quote, "'Tis better to have loved and lost than never to have loved at all."

When my father moved out, he left some of his clothes in our closets. Our house came with a room that could only be described as a dressing room, a square space that connected my bedroom and Julie's to our shared bathroom. It had two closets, built-in drawers, and a large mirror with big light bulbs all around it like a movie star's dressing room.

I would often open Julie's closet and stare at my father's button-up shirts and slacks and blazers, hanging limp, a cold reminder of what once had been. I would bring one shirt close to my face and take in the smell of musk and Brute aftershave. But more often than not, if the closet doors were open, I would walk past quickly, averting my eyes. The physical reminder of my father was too much at times.

A year after he returned to Israel, his temporary move became permanent. I don't remember my father telling us that he was not coming back to the U.S. except to visit. But I do remember helping him. In the summer of 1987, we took all his clothes that were hanging in our closets and stuffed them in suitcases and duffel bags. The four of us—my mother and sisters and I—took nine bags with us to Israel that year, six of which were full of my father's belongings.

In Frankfurt, Germany, where we had a layover, security searched every bag. Each time the agents opened another suitcase, the contents spilled out as if the bag had fallen off a car and was lying on the side of the road for anyone to see. Those were my father's clothes the security official was so callously sifting through. Did he not know what this meant? Did he not understand that we were collaborators in my father's break from his family? My mother and sisters and I were silent as the security agents performed their search.

The airport officials asked their normal gruff security questions: "Why are you going to Israel? Do you have family there? How long will you be there? Why is your father in Jerusalem?"

I felt nothing. I answered perfunctorily.

"To visit family. Three weeks. My father lives there."

When the last bag was packed back up and the zipper pulled all the way around, it was like a key turning in an echo chamber. The finality of the moment reverberated through my entire body. When it was my turn to get patted down by security, I didn't even do my usual grumbling. I had been hollowed out. My soul exposed. I had nothing left to give.

Animated Suspension
jeff burt

Scenario planning lists

1. We steal the truck, we get away, we deliver, we are paid $30K each.

2. We steal the truck, the Camry doesn't burn, we get caught by the cops, we go to jail.

3. Hadley cannot pull off her act of misdirection, Siciliano hits the guard but not hard enough, we cannot get away, we all go to jail.

4. Siciliano goes crazy, kills the guard, I take the truck with Hadley, make the drop, we get paid, Siciliano gets caught, he rats us out, we all go to jail.

5. Siciliano goes crazy, kills the guard, I leave Hadley, but ditch it on the side of the road, escape.

6. I take off before Hadley and Siciliano can get in, make the drop, the buyers round us up, we get buried in the muck of the delta.

I heard on the morning radio that if you plan different scenarios, you can begin to see the future in the paths, not just what you want it to be, and then you can proactively guide yourself in the right direction. The author cited generals, presidents, yogis, and business leaders, all who used scenario planning to pull their asses out of doomsday. The author first taught self-actualization, heaven and Christianity, mindfulness, and now visualizing scenarios. Kind of all the same thing.

In two mornings, I will drive a stolen Camry to steal a truck of legal medicinal marijuana with Hadley and Siciliano and take it to Modesto for a fence. In two mornings, I go to work for the first time in eighteen months, breaking the unendurable boredom that dangles in front of my face like a hypnotist's amulet, lulling me to death. In the age of "seize the day and do it now," I've had nothing to seize and do.

I grew up next to the Merced River, which starts in a frenzy up in Yosemite, where all that spring-melt water in a small rock-bound space creates white caps; a force that can kill, sweep boulders away, but then it gets out of the steep mountains and widens, flattens, becomes quiet, exhausted—that's what the rush of life started like, college, job, wife, kids, loss of job, loss of wife, loss of kids, and now flat, spread wide and motionless. I have become lonely, isolated, obsolete.

We are a sad gang of three, picked by Lobato not because I can drive a truck and Siciliano can be efficiently violent or Hadley because she's a grifter. We were chosen because I owed Lobato several thousand for drugs, Siciliano owed for drugs, a car, and destruction of Lobato's retail store, and Hadley because she was pregnant with his son's child.

Hadley is seventeen, pregnant, a con artist, without much of a sweet side. She believes in anything natural or organic, including not bathing. A survivalist, some might call her, except she's so young she has not had much to survive. A baby later and she'll change from noun to verb quickly.

Siciliano's a *did-that*. Whatever anyone's done in his or her life, he's done it too, and been worse at it. He's been fired from every job he's had, mostly for smoking weed at the counter, in the warehouse, or behind the business when he should have been working. He's crashed cars, his own and others, burned down his mother's house falling asleep with a lit cigarette, been a star athlete kicked off his teams before the season started, a short order cook, a sous chef, an addict, a recovering addict, and a relapsed addict. He's here because he can't do anything else.

I'm the new Tom Joad, updated into the 21st century, college-educated, father of two, divorced, and after forty, unable to land a full-time job. I'm here to rob a truck for a change of pace.

The three of us are Okies in truth, except for the state of origin, in transit, impoverished, weary of our souls groaning and our minds grappling with a world that has passed us like a bus you couldn't catch no matter how hard you ran, just when you thought it would wait on the corner it moved away, block after block, your hand reaching out, until you couldn't run any farther, and it gets lost in the crowd of traffic.

We check-in at a fishing resort Lobato arranged for us to spend two nights. The counter clerk doesn't laugh when Siciliano makes a crack about the Fifty First Dates poster with Drew Barrymore and Adam Sandler, says she heard it before, fifty times. She's old, heavy, wheezes like an old dog after climbing stairs, and gives us more than a once over. The resort has eight cabins. I cannot see another vehicle besides our tan Toyota Camry.

"I'll cut you guys some slack, seeing she's pregnant. Normally this rate is for three nights. I'll let it go at two nights. I've got one room with four beds, three mattresses and a cot. Made for weekend fishermen. It's cash for the room. I'm just gonna assume one of you is the father of that baby," she said staring at me.

Siciliano said, "He's her uncle. Do you have Wi-Fi?"

The clerk snorted. "Wi-Fi? Son, we don't even have a fax machine. You want to fish, we've got fish. If you want to do a little of this and a little of that, we've got fish. If you don't want to fish, we've got fish." She laughed and took us to the cabin, which turned out to have the space for three beds, the fourth stored upright against a window, a cot also stored upright, a sink, a bathroom, and room for two people to turn around, but not at that the same time. The cabin had the smell of dirt, hay, and perhaps horses. A graphic novel in Spanish lay on a cot. Migrants used the cabins, thus her obvious desire for cash.

"You know you need a guide to get on the delta in this spot, right? He'll have licenses for you if you don't have them. Costs $10 a head or $25 for the group. Includes the boat. You'll have to pay a buck or so for gas, too. Gilles. Name of the guide. Gilles LeBlanc. No mister. He lost the mister a long time ago. He thinks he's from the Louisiana Bayou but he's from by way of Clovis. Likes to act like a Cajun, but he ain't. His last name used to be Lawson. If he tries to get you to pay a disposal fee for the fish you catch, don't pay it. There is no disposal fee. Just tell him he can keep the fish and he'll be happy. He's a wise ass, but a small-time wise ass."

I'd been in a car all day, and a mattress, even if not supported by springs, felt very comfortable. For the first few hours, anyway, until my body started a permanent depression and the middle sagged, my neck cricked, and my feet discovered they were higher than my ears. Then I found myself listening for the sounds of the mosquitos and a painful, eerie stillness that I could tell floats over water. Crickets pulsed through the night so loudly I thought they could generate electricity. From over the water, I could hear a slide guitar, an occasional whoop and shout. I could smell cigarette smoke every twenty minutes wafting in the screen window near my bed. Siciliano was either lamenting the loss of his childhood, stroking the gray hairs, anguishing over his siblings, or devising some other family history to suit a conversation.

I rose. After sneaking out the front screen door and walking down to the water's edge in darkness, I flicked on the flashlight and looked out over the water. Fog was rising up to reach into the lichen hanging from the trees. It was not eerie like a sense of voodoo or evil, but eerie as if I was not meant to be there, the fog a warning sign, an omen, of something my mind would not be able to penetrate, this symbol of the water reaching up to pull down what it had given birth to.

A mutt came and lay down by my feet. His tongue kept flicking out of his mouth, as if telling me that he needed to eat. It was enough to send me back to the mattress, but a few minutes after I put the water out of my mind, the alarm went off, and we all awoke in the twilight to go fish. One dawn down, one left to go.

Gilles LeBlanc, our guide, says nothing. Siciliano and I pay for minnows and a thermos of coffee, and slide five five-dollar bills into his hand. Without a word, he puts poles and tackle in the boat, and sits in the middle. He has a shotgun in his left hand that he points straight up. Hadley sleeps in the chair back at the cabin.

"What do you need a shotgun for?" I ask.

"Later," he says, raising his chin to speak. I am not sure that he says *later* for he speaks in a tongue that is definitely not English. As he commands us to get in, Siciliano starts the trolling motor. We ignore the fog.

When the mist starts rising to about four feet over our heads, he has us put down our poles.

An enormous detonation shakes us.

He laughs. "Cherry bombs."

"It sounded like that was just up the way," I say.

He nods affirmatively. "Blows the fish to the top. Doesn't kill them directly. Stuns. Knocks 'em out. Just local boys fishin'."

We hear the roar of twin-engine boats in the distance.

He laughs. "Po-lice. Won't catch 'em. Got to catch 'em before the cherry bombs drop. They long gone with a full net."

When we stop, we notice that when he drinks straight from the thermos, a little pearl of coffee appears below his lower lip, suspends for a moment before dropping into his goatee and disappearing.

Where he motions to throw in the jigs, we catch small bass. If Le Blanc says nothing looking at our catch, and cocks his head as if in indecision, it means throw it back, to release it until it can grow until it fills up a griddle.

Around seven, the sun begins to poke through parts of the mist, we begin to see other boats. We hear an occasional muffled word here or there, a quiet motor perhaps forty yards away, though we never can see the fishermen. When the fog lifts, we begin to see a good many boats.

"Get your poles out of the water. Now," LeBlanc whispers.

"We're here to fish," Siciliano says.

"Get your poles out of the water. Oars, too. Make sure your line doesn't hang over the boat. Grab them cork bobbers. Thank god we got no worms. Pull the net."

He reaches back suddenly and pulls the trolling motor completely out of the water.

We obey, sullenly, and sit liked shamed boys, as if punished and not knowing why.

Gilles LeBlanc points out in the lake. "We're on sun-side. They want warmth and breakfast."

They are water moccasins, cottonmouths, swimming high in the water. They skim, their bodies almost fully apparent, as if they are being pulled along by some invisible string. Six, seven, eight come near the boat, looking like raiding parties in Egyptian boats high on the Nile.

"They'll crawl up your arm you put it in," LeBlanc laughs. "Want to try it, bluecoat? Some wise ass brought them into California. Not a native snake. Now's there's about thirty in the delta. We kill 'em as fast as we can."

That is it for me. We have caught eleven fish between us. We have two more hours to fish, but shotguns, cherry bombs, and non-native water moccasins combine to make me yearn for shore.

When we return early the clerk has coffee, and we gift the fish to Gilles. He does not say thanks. He proceeds to a stump and quickly starts gutting and cutting off the heads, and has filets faster than we could hitch our pants. Mosquitos buzz in rapid succession. Flies surround the fish guts.

"Gilles said you didn't like them snakes," the clerk says. "Once we had a truck driver stop here, he'd been pulling a two-nighter and was running empty and came by in the middle of the afternoon. He was working a sweat make a bottle of Coke proud. Wanted to go swimming, and he thought the pier would make a good point to dive into the water. Well, he dropped his trousers and took off a chain and there he was flying down the pier and then right before he took off, he saw one of them southern water snakes swimming at the end of the wood, and you know, he said that he took off and kept gyrating his legs and arms and yelling with a whoop of fear and just kept right on going, cleared the whole pond and landed on the other side. A case of animated suspension, he called it. Any you boys want to take a dip, let me know, and I'll go spot for you."

Siciliano lies in the bunk next to me, a simple bunk, as all bunks are, but this one has had a life that probably should have ended—the slats to support the mattress have bent to the weight of thousands and the legs splay out at an oblique degree, as if a deer on ice trying to stay upright. The only part of Siciliano's body above plumb level are his feet and shoulders, parallel anchors or girders preventing the bridge of his body from collapsing onto the lake of the floor. His head teeters near falling at a forty-five-degree angle toward the floor, lowering with every intake of breath, rising with every exhale, his Adam's apple alternating between garishly large and extra-large.

Hadley sleeps in a chair in nothing but underwear and bra, and appears the only one of us who is comfortable, her round belly raised like a roll in a hot oven. She has seventeen tats, one for each year of her life, and the simple cross tattoo on her belly has become like a landing strip crisscross as seen from the sky. She says angels land there.

Hadley has an unwanted pregnancy, though she is quite clear that she liked the guy and unprotected sex was consensual for both. Apparently, the childcare wasn't consensual and he split. She comes from Chowchilla, a dusty town, been in tiny shacks with no lawns her whole life, sometimes in the same bedroom as her folks, her father who lays irrigation piping, her mother who cleans stables. Her parents approved an abortion, did everything but put her on a table, but she liked that life grew in her since it didn't seem to grow outside of her. She's the one most excited about stealing a truck, has chattered for two days straight and, except for having money for blankets and baby books, doesn't have a thought for what she'll do with her share of $90,000.

Siciliano stirs, brushes back his black curly hair that by twenty-six already has gray streaking at the sideburns and running around the rim of the back of his nape. He has difficulty sleeping. He wanted out of the Army and tried multiple ways to obtain a general discharge. He rarely ironed his khakis, and wore khakis on the days dress blues were required. He performed poorly at his rather simple job of filing clerk. When break ended, he would reach for a cigarette and stay in the quad an additional five minutes, complaining that he needed to have a break from people. He says he got hooked on cigarettes so bad he was smoking three packs a day, headed to four. That's when he found weed, and cut his cigarette smoking in half. He says that with some measure of pride.

He succeeded in getting kicked out of the Army, the only thing he ever talks about that he was successful at. He grew up poor in Rhode Island, son of a single woman who did landscaping for a living, pulling the weeds for the rich, pulling up bulbs in June and replanting them in November, hands and knees work.

I keep imagining going to work. At eight, we'll hit the truck left idling for almost five minutes as the driver returns to the office to check his route, drink coffee, and flirt with the woman who runs the gate and sets the daily work schedule for the weed groomers and harvesters. Hadley will create the diversion by going to the office and talking to the gatekeeper and driver so that their backs will be facing the truck. I will walk in a 90-degree direction until out of view and then cut diagonally back and get in the driver's side. Siciliano will jack the driver's head when he exits the gatehouse, then run and get in the passenger side without closing the door, and then Hadley will end her conversation and she will squeeze in next to Siciliano and we'll be off. The whole plan counts on Siciliano knocking out the driver with one direct hit and the gatekeeper not noticing Hadley slip into the truck. We need at least twenty seconds to drive to the bottom of the hill where we can go left or right at the intersection and not be seen.

Whatever goodness lies ahead for us, whatever darkness, whatever punishment or grace, all starts now at dawn. Boredom has been broken. In the mist over the delta, everything pends. At dawn, it ends.

Do you believe in angels? she asks.

Normally that's a rhetorical question and the person keeps on talking, telling the other person whether angels exist.

But she cocks her head like a dog waiting for an answer.

No, not really, I answer, as if afraid that dog would bite.

What do you mean by *not really*? You mean a little, or you haven't made up your mind?

I mean, I stammer, that how could one really know.

By visitations. Which means you've never been visited by an angel.

And you have?

Yes. Most certainly. Several times. Twice with goodness, once with evil. You know, you can believe in angels without having had a visitation. There's thousands of scholars of the Bible and the Koran and the Torah, I think they call it, that haven't been visited but believe in angels.

They believe in many things they have not seen.

Seen? There's many things I have not seen, that many people have not seen, but I believe in them.

I'm sure you do.

But I've experienced them. You ever loved someone, and don't answer with the word *really* somewhere in your answer.

Yes, I have, I say.

How many times? Once, a hundred?

What does it matter?

Because if you said, like twelve, I'd know you've never been in love. If you said once or twice, then you know what love is.

I suppose now you're going to tell me that love and angels are like the same thing.

No, cuz they're not. But you can describe love in like eighty-six ways that two people interact, and then add in their emotions and you can get a description even if you can't see it, like an umbrella or a table. You don't think love is just chemistry, do you?

No, I don't believe it's just chemistry. But that does not make love like an angel. Love is not some imagination of a person.

No, it's more like an event. An angel. An angel is like an event.

I buy that.

So promise me something.

What's that?

In one day, when things start to happen, keep yourself open to angels, to the event. How you feel, not just what's happening in front of your eyes. Take it in like you would a lover. You'll get your visitation.

What if it's evil?

Evil's good, in a way, because the first experience you can acknowledge an angel means you can be open for more, and then a good angel can come to you.

She begins rubbing her belly in slow circles and lapses into a song that she keeps repeating about almonds and raisins and ponies.

Angels? Love? We were about to rip off a marijuana distributor with armed weapons. We were about to incur the wrath of a gangster's spider web with a little tug toward the edge that would send the spider in speed and deathly intentions in our directions. I did not believe in angels. But demons? Yes, I believed in demons.

Angels and demons. Self-actualization. Heaven. Scenario planning. Maybe it was all one and the same.

Hadley walks up the getaway road, making a large S as she saunters. She wears a tattered blue dress, no shoes, and looked like bugs had scattered their venom in half of her arms and legs. The scabs are bountiful. She's practicing her robbery routing.

She'll tell him she's a waif, a runaway, an orphan. She's got so many stories no one can keep track of them, least of all her. But she's practiced. One of the stories, any of the stories, will sell. She's like one of those one-person plays where she plays all the parts. Her story might be true, if you put them all together.

Abused by her mommy. Abused by her daddy. Her mommy and daddy died in a fire. She was left on the side of the road in Texas. She was a princess but her brothers pushed her out of the car and left her for dead.

Hadley's curved and exposed. Like watching a cat preen, the driver will become mesmerized by her hand stroking her hair. All he will see will be her hand stroking, feel his growing lust, and then Siciliano will move in from the back and bust his head. The guy will go down without stagger, the hit will be so hard. Siciliano will pick up the keys. Then I will drive us three to a T in the road down a hill where we will be out of sight and make a turn left though the they'll think we turned right toward the interstate. Then we will drive on three county roads until we hit Ripon, where we will park the truck in a vacant warehouse that once served as an enormous vegetable freezer, move the jars, bags, pouches, and bricks to two different cars. A man will show and pay us ninety thousand dollars. Then we'll walk out the door.

Second dawn. It's the day the hypnotist's pendulum comes to a stop. It's the day the awful suspended present goes into motion again.

I look at the lake, with only a few patches left of fog evaporating and lingering over the water.

Animated suspension—the act of everyone except the rich and powerful, scrambling all limbs to stay above destitution, catastrophe, the mindless inanimate poverty of soul, the whirling of legs and arms to stay beyond the reach of snakes as they try to climb up the wood, to leap beyond them, to avoid the fall into demons.

In my head, as I grip the steering wheel of the Camry, Hadley has already turned and is walking toward the car. Siciliano is lighting a cigarette, his leg bouncing from a nervous foot.

I want to take off my shirt, my socks and shoes, remove my wallet and keys. I want to sprint down the pier, and when my head appears out of the water, I expect to hear clapping, applause, as if at a baptism. I want to be new.

But I don't. Siciliano pays the resort clerk. She gives him a stank eye and tells him to be careful about his next step. Gilles grunts as he passes, smiles for the first time.

It will all go as planned. Hadley will work her magic, drawing attention. Siciliano will knock out the guard with a single hit. Hadley will come running. Siciliano, high on adrenaline, will stand over the guard, shaking, spittle falling from his lips. I will have taken command of the truck. Hadley will come up behind Siciliano and take the baseball bat from his hands, and then, and then the hypnotist's pendulum stops, stops dead in the air as the baseball bat crushes Siciliano's head, as she has told me, but I will drive the truck down the driveway without Hadley, her womb bouncing in my rear view mirror, shaking the bat and screaming. In one seemingly spontaneous moment of time, I will deprive of her fortune and create escape. I will save her life. I will have planned a future, and it will not be mine.

I want to tell Hadley that I alone will end up dead, buried in the muck of the delta, that I alone will be buried where the water moccasins gather. I want to tell Hadley that I have learned in one single moment of time, when the pendulum has suspended, when time no longer ticks, I will have been both demon and angel. I want to tell her I believe.

poem

Shade

joshua mckinney

A man thinks he owns his form,
           that his shadow is his alone,
that his body, its flesh and bone,
           obstructs the light in his image,
when in fact, he possesses nothing.
           The shadow casts the man.

A Deep Earnestness in Her Speech

leonard crosby

In 2013, shortly before I left San Francisco due to rising rents, I went on the saddest date of my life. It was a sign of the terrible ways the city was transforming, along with my own foibles, and the need to change and grow into a better person.

She came into the Uptown with two sad-looking guys, both of whom I easily beat at pool. Afterwards, playing against my friend Nick, I watched her, trying to find the right moment to introduce myself. She was petite and dressed in an indie-look I knew from the 90s. Big black frames and a brown cardigan over an orange-white checkered button up.

In the middle of one of my shots, she got up to put some music on the jukebox. When the distinctive twang of "Rebel, Rebel" came on, I told her too loudly that I liked her choice. She wheeled around, startled. Walking back to my game, I knocked over my pool cue. Before I could grab it, she picked it up and handed it to me.

After her boys left and I lost to Nick, we sat down. Her name was Holly, she used to live in the Mission. She was a filmmaker now in Indiana, out in San Francisco visiting friends.

"What's your film about?" I asked

"I can't tell you that. It's a secret."

I laughed. I would tell people about the novel I was writing all the time.

We talked about movies. I asked whether someday American major films would become like the 1950s again, relying on acting and not spectacle. She shook her head.

"The thing is, the acting in those is so good, so determined, you can't reproduce it. They'll never make films like that again. The shit you hear about Hollywood actors today, they don't take themselves seriously." Her small brown eyes flashed behind her glasses. An exception, she continued, was Daniel Day Lewis.

I told her about an article I'd read on the making of *There Will Be Blood*. Lewis terrified crew and cast by remaining in character as Daniel Plainview on and off the set. Between scenes interns would offer him water or coffee and he'd look at them like he was going to eat them.

"That's what I mean," she said. "Brando, Bogart, Audrey Hepburn, they did that as a matter of course. If you're going to be seen by millions of people, take your job seriously."

I listened very closely, the rest of the bar fading into a blur. I lost track of Nick and the pool game. Holly had straight brown hair, and a short nose. She was thin, and her skinny jeans could have fit a teenage boy. She was plain, really, and looked like any hipster white girl you might meet in the Mission, but her moxie reminded me of my first girlfriend. I liked her opinions about movies, and her dedication to making them. At some point she got up to get drinks. Nick sat, taking a break from his game.

"You're not actually going after that, are you?"

"No, just good conversation," I lied.

"You should go talk to that girl," he said, nodding across the room at a young curvy rocker.

"I should."

When Holly came back with our beers, Nick returned to his game and Holly and I talked about hip-hop. She knew female underground rappers, had seen shows I'd wanted to go to but missed. She had a deep earnestness in her speech, like she was angry at something and could only rectify it through serious conversation. Her words came out concise and focused, like a poet trying to bare her life to an audience. I found this attractive and assumed she wanted me as her confidant. She told me she was only in town for two more days, then she was flying back to Indiana. I started forming a narrative for the rest of the night in my mind.

Nick left, and a rowdy group of early-twenty-somethings came in and started singing, "I Love Rock and Roll" with the jukebox. Holly glared at them.

"I can't stand that. You wanna to go dancing?"

"Sure," I said, glancing at the group of girls, trying to figure out what was upsetting her.

We made our way through the crowd. Outside Holly immediately took my arm in hers. I grinned at this and halfway to Mission Street I pulled her aside and took her hands. I looked down at her, keeping my face serious.

"Holly, there's something I want to tell you."

She let go of my hands.

"Wow, why are you getting weird on me?" she said, cocking her head away and narrowing her eyes.

"What? No, I…Never mind, let's go."

We went to The Beauty Bar, a tiny, trashy dance club on the corner of 19th and Mission. It was packed. Inside the door, I asked if she still wanted to dance. She nodded. We got glasses of whiskey with the last of my cash. Holly wasn't all that pleased with it. But fueled by the fumes, I said the line I'd tried to say out on the street.

"Holly, I've been trying very hard not to kiss you tonight."

In the loud bar I couldn't hear her response, but her quizzical look told me I'd blown it. Still, that look of confusion was all the rejection I got. She still wanted to dance.

We moved onto the floor, but now her face looked pinched, strained. When I put an arm around her, or danced behind her, she didn't object, but she was hardly moving and looked bored. At some point I asked if she wanted to go, and she nodded.

"It was just so fucking packed in there," she said outside.

Crossing Mission, moving up 19th towards Valencia, I asked, "Where are you at right now? Like in relationships?"

"It's complicated."

"So, you're seeing someone."

"Like I said, it's complicated."

I thought I knew what this meant. She was seeing someone or was still in love with someone. I decided to ignore it.

"It's so much easier, isn't it, when you first fall in love," I said. "You're so innocent, you don't hesitate because you haven't been hurt before."

"Yeah," she said. Her voice dropped.

As we moved down the street, she explained where she was staying, which turned out to be only a few blocks from my house in the Panhandle. I asked if she wanted to go home and drink.

"No," she said. "I still want to dance."

We walked down Valencia trying to find a place. I didn't realize how far down we'd gone until we came to Amnesia and took a look inside. There was a cover. I told the bouncer we weren't interested. Holly asked if we could go inside and hear the music before deciding to pay or not.

We went in. "I don't have any more cash," I said.

"I know," she spat back. "You told me already."

I stood there, eying the room while she paid the cashier. I was beginning to wish I'd left with Nick.

I turned to the bar while she talked with the cashier about the band. I thought I could at least order drinks if not pay for them. Behind the counter a tall blond woman was serving. She looked angry, constantly harried for booze. After a minute I realized it was my friend Jordan from the California College of the Arts, where I'd done my MFA. She didn't notice me until I ordered.

"Hey, Leonard," she said, a smile on her face. "Nice to see you."

When Holly came up and offered money for the beers, Jordan said, "No, these are on the house. Nice seeing you, man."

As I handed Holly her beer, Jordan smirked at me before turning back to serving.

There was more space on this dance floor, more gay boys, and fewer drunk girls in their twenties. Holly started dancing and her face looked almost happy. While we danced, she kept taking my hand and raising it up above our heads, as if to let some invisible couple dance under our hand arch. I thought, *this has to mean something*. You don't hold hands with someone you just met, *unless*. We danced until we were sweaty, and our beers were gone, then we moved back outside to the cold air.

I asked if we were catching a cab.

"Of course," she said.

I thought of having another drink in her kitchen. Making eggs, watching a movie, maybe. At this point I really didn't want sex. She hadn't kissed me. I was tired. If I'd been more sober or less lonely, I would have made the right decision immediately: left from there and taken the bus home. But I felt drawn to her. She was crossing signals, and I wanted to know what that meant.

Halfway through the taxi ride home, she stopped talking. Her face scrunched up, like she'd been hiding a migraine all night and couldn't go on faking. I asked what was wrong.

"My father just died," she said. "I've been taking care of him for years in Indiana, he just passed while I was here in San Francisco."

"Oh, Holly, I'm so sorry."

I hugged her. She didn't cry, though tears welled, and she shook her head. I felt a blush of embarrassment about trying to kiss her earlier. At the same time, I felt sympathy for what she was going through, I also thought: *this girl's got some issues. Why would you go out with a stranger when your father just died?* Then I immediately felt guilty for thinking it. I've yet to lose anyone close, and I wanted in that moment to empathize with someone who had. I have no faith in an afterlife. Death to me isn't a transformation, just a barren loss. Only the sharing of stories about the person who has passed provides any solace. I didn't really know Holly; she wasn't going to tell me stories about her father. She'd laid her pain out for me and I struggled to find the words to make sense of it.

"I didn't know, Holly," I said. "I'm so sorry."

"It's OK," she said. "He was a bastard anyway."

I hugged her again.

We got to Fell St. and the driver stopped. I got up, took Holly's hand. She let go and I realized she wasn't going with me.

"I thought…"

"No, you're getting out here, I'm going home."

"But…"

"No. Go home, Leonard. Call me."

I got out, hung my head. As I walked home, I thought about what she was going through. Even if she hated her father, that made the loss no less. Knowing that the person who was supposed to love you but had mistreated you instead, and would never fix what they'd done, might be even worse. I wondered again why she'd gone out. When my own father dies, I imagine myself in a bar only if drunk and supported by my brother and sister. Ruining a black suit with tears and whiskey spills. If Holly hated her father and was on vacation, I could almost see it, but why hadn't she left with her friends? To try and find comfort in a boy she hardly knew was a faith in strangers I couldn't comprehend.

I called Holly as soon as I assumed she'd made it home. No answer. I sent her a text before going to sleep:

Holly, I apologize for being so forward. I had a wonderful time hanging out with you. I didn't know what you were going through. I'd like to see you again. I hope you're OK tonight.

She never responded.

Issue 10 Contributors

Tanner Abernathy teaches high school English and coaches judo in Federal Way, a Seattle suburb pleasantly named after the highway that bisects it. He writes image-centric poetry and fiction, enjoys walking with his wife, and caring for his cat and rabbits. His writing has appeared in *Abyss & Apex*, *HASH* (forthcoming), and *Jeopardy Magazine*.

Zoë Ballering teaches writing and writes radio ads in Bellingham, Washington. She holds an MFA in fiction from Western Washington University.

Eric Bryan is a freelance writer originally from Burlingame Hills, California. His nonfiction, fiction and verse have been published in *The Saturday Evening Post*, *The London Magazine*, *The Globe and Mail* and many others in North America, Europe, Australia, New Zealand and Hong Kong.

Jeff Burt lives in Santa Cruz County, California, and works in mental health. He has contributed to *Ecotheo Review*, *Per Contra*, *Bird's Thumb*, and *The Nervous Breakdown*. He won the *Consequence Magazine* 2016 Fiction prize.

Laton Carter's short fiction has appeared in *Atticus Review*, *The Hoosier Review*, *Indiana Review*, *Necessary Fiction*, and *Shirley Magazine*. Carter works as an educational assistant in a middle school.

Leonard Crosby received his MFA from the California College of the Arts, and his work has appeared in *Eleven Eleven*, *Forklift: Ohio*, and the *Oakland Review*. He currently works as an Assistant Professor in English and humanities at Cogswell University in San Jose, and as editor for the school's literary magazine, www.cogzine.com. More of his work can be found at: www.leonardcrosby.com.

Paul Curley is the son of a fire chaser. In the 1970's, his dad used to pack six kids into a station wagon and follow the plumes of California wildfires. Now Paul lives with his wife and two daughters in Portland, Oregon, where he teaches English as a second language. He doesn't chase fires. Paul's fiction has appeared in magazines such as *The Madison Review*, *Gravel*, *The Timberline Review*, *Shout Out UK*, and *Widdershins*.

Lawrence Di Stefano is a poet and photographer. He is currently an MFA Poetry candidate at San Diego State University. He lives in San Diego.

Halina Duraj's stories have appeared in *The Harvard Review*, *The Sun*, *Fiction*, and *The O. Henry Prize Stories*. Her debut story collection, The Family Cannon, was published by Augury Books in 2014. She teaches literature and creative writing at the University of San Diego.

Stephanie Barbé Hammer is a 6-time Pushcart Prize nominee in fiction, nonfiction and poetry with work published in *The Bellevue Literary Review*, *Hayden's Ferry Review*, *Pearl*, the *James Franco Review*, *Isthmus*, *Cafe Irreal*, and the *Gold Man Review*. She is the author of the prose poem chapbook SEX WITH BUILDINGS (dancing girl press), the full-length collection HOW FORMAL? (Spout Hill Press), the fabulist novel THE PUPPET TURNERS OF NARROW INTERIOR (Urban Farmhouse Press) and the magical realism craft book DELICIOUS STRANGENESS (Spout Hill Press). Her novelette RESCUE PLAN is forthcoming with Bamboo Dart Press in February 2021

Amanda Laughtland is the author of Postcards to Box 464 (Bootstrap Press). She teaches English in the suburbs of Seattle and enjoys creating zines and books through her super-small publishing project, Teeny Tiny Press. She wrote "Alphabet" for Lexi.

Alice Lowe writes about life and literature, food and family. Her essays have been published in numerous literary journals, including *Ascent*, *Baltimore Review*, *South 85 Journal*, and *Hobart*. Her work has been cited in the Best American Essays and nominated for Pushcart Prizes and Best of the Net. She also has written extensively on the life and work of Virginia Woolf. Alice lives in San Diego, California and can be read at www.alice-loweblogs.wordpress.com.

Jessica Mehta is a multi-award-winnin poet and author of several books. As a citizen of the Cherokee Nation, space, place, and ancestry inform much of her work. You can find Jessica at www.jessicamehta.com, on IG @thisCherokeeRose, or on Twitter @CherokeeRoseUp.

Joshua McKinney's most recent book of poetry, Small Sillion (Parlor Press, 2019), was short-listed for the 2019 Golden Poppy Award and is currently a nominee for the Northern California Book Award. His work has appeared in such journals as *Boulevard, Denver Quarterly, Kenyon Review, New American Writing*, and many others. He is the recipient of The Dorothy Brunsman Poetry Prize, The Dickinson Prize, The Pavement Saw Chapbook Prize, and a Gertrude Stein Award for Innovative Writing.

Shira Musicant has made Santa Barbara home for over forty years. She no longer roller skates, but reads, writes, hikes, dances, cooks, protests, and gardens. When she is not so occupied, she is a somatic psychotherapist and an adjunct professor at Antioch University Santa Barbara. Her writing can be found in the *Santa Barbara Literary Journal, Two Hawks Quarterly*, and *Literally Stories*.

Laura Picklesimer writing has been featured in *Riprap, Bookwoman* and the *Santa Ana River Review*, among other publications. She was the grand prize winner of Enizagam Journal's 2018 Fiction Contest, won Arch Street Press's 2019 First Pages Prize and received third place in the Women's National Book Association's 2018 YA Fiction Contest. Laura studied creative writing at UCLA and earned her MFA from Cal State Long Beach. She teaches English at Chaffey College.

Timothy Pilgrim is a Pacific Northwest poet and 2018 Pushcart Prize nominee. He has several hundred acceptances from journals such as *Seattle Review, Third Wednesday, Santa Anna River Review, Windsor Review, San Pedro River Review, Toasted Cheese*, and *Hobart*. He is author of Mapping Water.

Lois Rosen joyfully leads Salem, Oregon's Trillium Writers, the I.C.L. Writing Workshop at Willamette University, and co-founded the Peregrine Poetry Group. She won the Willamette Writers' Conference 2016 Kay Snow Fiction Award and had her story performed by the Portland Liars' League. Her poetry books are Pigeons (Traprock Books) and Nice and Loud (Tebot Bach). Her work has been published in over a hundred journals, including *Gold Man Review*.

Claire Scott is an award-winning poet who has received multiple Pushcart Prize nominations. Her work has been accepted by the *Atlanta Review, Bellevue Literary Review, New Ohio Review, Enizagam* and *Healing Muse* among others. Claire is the author of Waiting to be Called and Until I Couldn't. She is the co-author of Unfolding in Light: A Sisters' Journey in Photography and Poetry.

Sherry Shahan lives in a laid-back beach town in California where she grows carrot tops in ice cube trays for pesto. Her novel in free verse Purple Daze: A Far Out Trip, 1965 features a tumultuous year in history. Shorter work has appeared in Oxford University Press, Los Angeles Times, Exposition Review, Confrontation, The Writer and forthcoming from F(r)iction. She holds an MFA from Vermont College of Fine Arts.

Melissa Siig is an award-winning journalist and editor based in Tahoe City, Calif. Her articles have appeared in Nevada Magazine, ESPN.com, Alaska Airlines Magazine, the Reno-Gazette Journal, and SKIING. Her story "Tahoe Magic," was published in 2012 in the anthology "Tahoe Blues" (Bona Fide Books). When not working on her memoir, "All of Our Goodbyes Are Yours," she is busy wrangling her three children and large German shepherd, and running a one-screen movie theater with her husband.

Charlie J. Stephens is a non-binary writer living in Northern California. Charlie has lived all over the U.S. as a bike messenger, wilderness guide, book seller, and seasonal shark diver (for educational purposes only). Charlie's work has appeared in Peculiar, Hinterland, Fresh.Ink, Prometheus Dreaming, Flexible Persona, and Forge Literary Magazine, among others. Charlie is currently working on a collection of short stories. More at charliejstephenswriting.com and on Instagram @charliejstephenswriting.

Andrew Stevens is a Seattle-based writer who specializes in self-deprecating flash nonfiction with a defeatist worldview. His work has been published in The Journal of Compressed Creative Arts, The Bookends Review, and nowhere else, due in large part to long-standing depression, insecurity, and laziness.

Max Talley was born in New York City and lives in Southern California. His fiction and essays have appeared in Fiction Southeast, Vol.1 Brooklyn, Entropy, Santa Fe Literary Review, Gravel, Atticus Review, and Litro. Talley's novel, Yesterday We Forget Tomorrow, was published in 2014, and Delirium Corridor, an anthology of dark fiction is forthcoming in November. He is associate editor for Santa Barbara Literary Journal. www.maxdevoetalley.com

Emily Townsend is a recent graduate from Stephen F. Austin State University. Her works have appeared in cream city review, Superstition Review, The Account, Noble / Gas Qtrly, Santa Clara Review and others.

A nominee for a Pushcart Prize, Best American Essays, and Best of the Net, she is currently tinkering with essays and poems in Eugene, Oregon.

Katherine Van Eddy is a California-born poet living in Sumner, WA. She earned a BA in Creative Writing and MAT in Elementary Education and is currently working towards an MFA from the Rainier Writing Workshop. Her poems have appeared in Gold Man Review, Creative Colloquy, Clover, and Cirque. She has two cute kids, teaches 5th grade, and enjoys being outside whenever possible.

Ashley Warren is a Minnesota native living in Cambria, California. This piece is an excerpt from an unpublished memoir titled Oasis for Everything. Her work has appeared in several print and online publications including Packingtown Review, Hiram Poetry Review, Santa Clara Review, Red River Review, Roanoke Review, and Sandy River Review. Her first book, Tiny Coffins, was published by Open Book Press, 2018.

Anna Genevieve Winham writes at the crossroads of science and the sublime, cyborgs and the surreal. She is Ninth Letter's 2020 literary award winner in Literary Nonfiction, Writer Advice Flash Fiction Contest's 2020 3rd place winner, and was long-listed for the 2020 Penrose Poetry Prize. Anna serves as the Prose Editor for Passengers Journal, and she writes and performs with the Poetry Society of New York, moonlighting as Velvet Envy in The Poetry Brothel. You can find her poetry in Q/A Poetry, Panoplyzine, Meniscus, Breadcrumbs Magazine, Wild Roof Journal, and others. Her prose appears or is forthcoming in Tilde~, Oxford Public Philosophy, Rock & Sling, Paragraph, The Radical Art Review, and Passengers Journal. While attending Dartmouth College (which was the pits), she won the Stanley Prize for experimental essay and the Kaminsky Family Fund Award.

Kirby Michael Wright's new book is THE QUEEN OF MOLOKA'I, a true story adventure based on the life and times of his Hawaiian grandma.

Gogo Zoger is a writer and creator, inspired by nature and time as a creative template. Studying Creative Writing and Dance at Loyola Marymount University in sunny Los Angeles, she is a passionate artist hoping to write my way through life, and save the planet while doing so.

www.ingramcontent.com/pod-product-compliance
Lightning Source LLC
Chambersburg PA
CBHW051847170626
46807CB00003B/1384